Mohammed Abdullah Ibrahim

THE HEIR OF MERIDIAN

AUSTIN MACAULEY PUBLISHERS™

LONDON * CAMBRIDGE * NEW YORK * SHARJAH

ISBN – 9789948755159 – (Paperback)
ISBN – 9789948755166 – (E-Book)

Application Number: MC-10-01-6967981
Age Classification: 17+

Printer Name: iPrint Global Ltd
Printer Address: Witchford, England

First Published 2024
AUSTIN MACAULEY PUBLISHERS FZE
Sharjah Publishing City
P.O Box [519201]
Sharjah, UAE
www.austinmacauley.ae
+971 655 95 202

Plot

3

An immortal is sent on a task from the great world of Meridian to the world of humans (earth) to find the Jewel of Meridian. The task is necessary to make him ascend to the throne of Meridian and be the next king of the immortals' world.

During his task, he will face a lot of difficult circumstances. Especially as he is new in this world, losing his powers and falling in love with a human girl will make his mission very hard to achieve. The events follow, and he will be forced to choose between his love and the throne of Meridian. He also must find a way to deal with guardians interfering, regardless of all the difficulties he already has. So what will he do to save his dignity and not lose his love?

For those eight characters who inspired me and shaped the inspirational world of mine.

Prologue

We know that Meridian is an imaginary great circle on our planet's surface, but what is the reason behind this name? Where has the name come from?

Very faraway in this universe, and in the center of it, there is Meridian, the wondrous world of immortals, where the sky is dark blue and there are many different creatures living there, ruled by a single king and queen. The rulers of the immortals' world and this world controls all the worlds secretly, but in the last 3000 years, this world has separated itself from the others by a veil because the immortals in this world have suffered enough from human greed, so they created the veil and put the guardians with magical powers to protect the veil and continue the peaceful life. Once every thousands of years, a new king comes to rule the great world of Meridian.

A beautiful green space, some giant creatures with small ones, and flying palaces with beautiful clouds—they all lived in peace in this magical world. And the immortals are living for eternity. Some of them have been born from the marriage of two immortals, and some are founded from nature—the air, water, fire, and earth.

The immortals watching what is happening on earth and in other worlds feel pity and the misery humans are suffering from. The world of Meridian and the magical veil draw their powers from the Jewel of Meridian, a great jewel founded with the birth of our universe, consisting of great and mighty power carried by the king of Meridian. When a new king comes to sit on the throne, the previous king must send him a task, and before that, he sends the Jewel of Meridian to the earth and sends the new heir to find it and accomplish the task. With every previous king, the experiences were different from the others because when the jewel is sent to the earth, it's protected by the guardians, the same guardians who protect the veil between the worlds. They live in the world of humans, hidden among ordinary people. Their task is to preserve the jewel and give it to the new king when he comes to take it. Alongside guardians, there is a strain of humans that vowed to serve the immortals over ages.

The heir's mission is specified, but the experience in the human world is different from one king to another! The new heir's mission is difficult this time because the world of humans has changed massively since a thousand years ago.

Chapter One
It Begins

A sound like an old clock rang 12 times; everyone noticed the sky color has changed. Everyone in Meridian knew what that meant. The creatures gathered. The immortals were curious about this moment. The king of Meridian sent his counselor to tell his son, the next king, that the time has come.

Prince Arkon, the next king, was resting as usual in the hot lake in his palace. He also noticed the sky while he was concerned. A dark blue-purple hole opened in the air. Arkon flew out of the water and walked toward that hole. It was one of the gates that allowed the crossing between the worlds. He saw something like this before in the Infinite City in Meridian, but it was thousands of years ago. Once he crossed the gate, everything changed. He looked behind him, and the gate was gone. The air is totally different. The sky's light-blue color was a new color; the clouds were white, and the sunlight was extreme on his fluffy skin. He raised his hand in front of his eyes to block the sunlight, looked around, and saw the green trees everywhere, like he was in a forest. He realized that the signs were for the heir's mission, but he couldn't know how he arrived at the earth in a flash. Arkon tried to fly to see the area around him, but he couldn't even raise his leg from the ground. His body started to shake; his powers had vanished. He began to walk and walk among the woods. He saw water on the side edge of the woods. He went closer to see; it was like an island surrounded by water and other close islands. He kept walking until he saw houses far away. He kept moving, and when Arkon almost arrived at the first cottage, he fainted and fell on the ground.

After long hours, Arkon opened his eyes slowly. He was confused because this was the first time that he had lost consciousness. He looked around to see the place and found himself in a small cottage. The fryers hung above the wooden table; the eggs and fruits were in a wooden bowl on the table; the curtains were almost close; and a small amount of sunlight barely entered from the window that overlooked the seawater. He pushed himself away from the old sofa.

An old woman put her hands on him. He freaked out. She said, "Don't worry, I found you on the ground, and I recognized you immediately!"

Arkon asked, "Do you know who I am?"

"Yes, of course, I know you. I knew that the gate was opened earlier this morning, and I know that we are waiting for a new king to come to do his mission!"

He asked, "And who are you? How did you know? And where am I?"

The old woman smiled and said, "Take a breath first, and I will explain everything to you." She walked to the sink and brought a cup of water. When she approached him, he raised his hands and stopped her.

Then he said, "If you know me, you would know that I don't drink or eat because I'm an immortal!"

The old woman replied, "Yes, I know, but somehow you lost your powers when you crossed the gate, and then I found you fainted. That's why you need to drink and eat like humans. I don't know if that is part of the task or not, but it's happened, and it's the first time for me to see that because that didn't happen with the previous kings when they came to accomplish their tasks!"

Arkon was shocked and immediately asked, "Are you here since the last king's mission?"

"No, I'm here from the first king's mission. My name is Halinor, and I was born to help the kings cross between the worlds, especially when they didn't have the Jewel of Meridian. When your father came to earth to find the jewel, we were on the other part of the earth, but in the last hundred years, the gate changed its place to here. We are on an island called the Princess Islands. This place is beautiful. I changed my form to acclimatize with the people here. You asked me before about how I knew you; believe me, all the people who will see you will doubt that you are a human being because the face you carry will tell them that you are an angel or a god, depending on their culture."

Arkon asked, "Where shall I go now? Where is the Jewel of Meridian?"

Halinor answered, "The answer to this question is on the map!"

"Which map?" the prince asked.

"The magical map of the jewel! Did you lose it?"

"No, I didn't because I didn't bring any map with me."

Halinor replied, "Your Highness, do you have the instructions? Wait, how did you even come here?"

"Well, I was in the hot lake in my palace, and I heard the sounds in the sky like an old clock sound that rang 12 times. Then the sky's color changed, and my heart started beating fast, so I knew that it was the sign for the next king. So, I got out of the water, and a hole opened next to me, and I was attracted to it. Then I ended here in your cottage."

Halinor stood and walked next to the window and said, "This is happening for the first time. The gate was very fast with you. It usually takes many days until the gate opens in Meridian to get the new king across. At this time, I'm sure that the king will find a way to open another port and send you the map to the jewel and send you one of your servants to help you with your task. Maybe finding the jewel will not be hard; the harder thing is to find the guardians of the veil because they protect the jewel, and they are hidden very well in the human world. If you live long enough in the immortal world, you will not find it difficult to recognize them."

Arkon stated, "I lived more than 4100 years, and yes, I know them very well. They were my friends."

Halinor stared at Arkon's eyes directly and said, "I remembered an old prophecy, and I hope this one would mean you!"

Arkon asked, "Which prophecy?"

Halinor answered, "I'm not sure about that, Your Highness. I'm not sure yet." Then she said, "Stay here, Your Highness. I will go buy you new clothes that humans wear these days to make you cope very well with them. I'm afraid that you will be forced to stay here for a few days until they find a way to open the new gate, and then you will be able to cross another country in this world to find what you are looking for." Then she got out and left the house.

The heir stood and walked to explore the place; he then saw a mirror that was hung on the wall. He stared at himself, then panicked. His moon face was still the same, but his long hair had changed. He took a few minutes and said, "Why didn't I think to cut it like this before?" A white face, beautiful brown eyes, and dark black hair, and with his royal tall stature, he was like the most beautiful creature in this world.

Chapter Two
A Strange Visitor

A spiritual mediator came to me and told me about a message from the immortals on our planet. A psychiatrist on her desk was writing on her laptop and listening to the man who sat in front of her and was uttering insane things. The man yelled, "Why me? Why they choose me rather than the Americans?"

The doctor replied with a pale expression, "Yes, why, I wonder too!"

The man stared into the doctor's eyes and exploded, "Why don't you believe me? I'm telling the truth." Then he started uttering a different language and breaking the decoration stuff on her desk. She pressed the emergency button, and the sound started in all the medical clinic. Immediately after, a male nurse entered and pulled the man out of the room. Then he began to talk in his insane language to make the patient feel comfortable.

The young doctor sighed and put her apron in a paper bag. The nurse came back to her room. She asked, "How did you control him?"

The nurse answered, "I have watched him many times talking in this strange language, so I learned from him for a situation like that."

She looked at him and said, "You are better than me." Then she sat on her chair. "I can't deal with him anymore. Tell his family to change his doctor."

"No, are you giving up?"

"Giving up? What are you talking about? He's been my patient for one year, and there is no progress in his therapy. Do you think it's easy to admit that I can't fix him?"

"I'm sorry," the nurse responded. Then he put a group of envelopes on her desk and said, "All these envelopes are to remind you about paying the bank's loan because we are late on the deposit date as usual."

The doctor whined, "I think they will close the clinic very soon if we don't pay the interest for them." She sighed.

Then the nurse said, "Do you want to drink with me?"

She stared at him. "Why shall I drink with you?" She thought for a minute and remembered that she had no one else to drink with.

They ended up together in a small restaurant to drink and eat at night. The nurse, who was her friend, took out a piece of paper. "I forgot to give you this. This paper is for your small land in Ironwood. It's not sold yet, right?" the nurse asked.

"No, who would buy a faraway land that contains a massive amount of bad soil and rocks? I don't know why I inherited it from my family. It's worthless."

"We delayed paying the rent, and also, we spent half of the rent deposit. What shall we do?"

"By the way, why are you still working with me? You can quit this job."

"I want to repay all the kindness and generosity that I got from your father."

"I don't want to listen. Shut up," she interrupted.

"By the way, are you still dreaming of leaving the country permanently?"

"Yes. Once I pay all my debts, I will leave," she replied.

"Oh, Arya, please find a guy to pay your debts instead of you!"

She stared angrily at him and barked, "I don't like to depend on someone else."

He replied, "Is that what really prevents you, or are you just not liked by men!"

"How dare you! I even got a huge diamond ring from a friend, but I rejected him." She stood, hit him with her bag, and left him.

Out in a random park, the psychiatrist Arya took a small spade and dug under a big tree, searching for something. She kept digging until she saw something shining. She took it out of the ground. "Finally, I found the ring. I told that idiot I got that from a man. Why didn't he believe me? Oh, my ring, I found you because you are destined to be mine. Oh, I can't believe that his name was Caleb. What a child name is that? However, it does not matter. What matters is that I can pay all my bills and the rent for a few months by selling this ring." She took out her necklace and saw what was drawn on the necklace's back: the island that she dreamed of living on. She raised her head to the sky, and the darkness had covered the clouds. Three stars were shining clearly in the sky; the park was empty; and the air was flawless with trees breezing. She saw something move fast in the sky. She thought it was a star. Suddenly, a dark blue-purple hole opened in front of her.

A strange man with funny features came out of this hole. Arya couldn't believe what she just saw. She immediately uttered, "Oh my god! I'm just crazy like my patients." Then she fainted; the man caught her head and put it smoothly on the ground. He saw her apron in the bag, and he immediately took it because he was naked. The man spoke.

"I'm sorry, I must take it. I will find a way to bring it back to you." Then he left in a hurry.

When Arya woke up minutes later, she found herself on the ground. She slowly stood and looked around. She saw that her apron was gone and thought that someone had hit her and taken the apron with the ring in its pocket. She felt that was the reason why she did not remember what happened.

In the meantime, in another part of the world, Arkon was at Halinor's cottage. She sat in front of him, then she suddenly said, "Your Highness, the gate opened on another place on earth." Arkon stood.

"Where? What shall I do?"

Halinor answered, "Another gate opened in the place where you came from last time. Let's go." They both rushed to the woods to find the magical gate. When they arrived at the gate, Halinor said, "Your Highness, this gate will lead you to another country on earth, and I think you will see your servant. I feel that they sent someone from Meridian. I want you to take the map and find the jewel. I want to give you one single piece of advice: please don't underestimate your happiness. You don't know, but maybe living a few years as a human is better than living immortally."

Arkon replied, "I don't understand what you mean by that." Halinor waved with her hand that held a silver ring with a tree sign on it, and the air pushed the heir into the gate.

Then he listened to her words like a whisper: "You will know once your heart is filled with love."

When Arkon crossed the gate, he arrived at another place. He saw the trees everywhere, so he thought that he was also in another forest. A strong voice called him from behind. Arkon recognized the voice immediately. It was his loyal servant, Tynar's voice. "My Lord, the next king of Meriden, I'm blessed to see you," Tynar said.

Arkon stared at him, hid that he was happy to see him, and asked, "Why you delayed that much? And where are we right now?"

"My king, there are many things that happened. It's different this time; everything is different than the last time. I even lost the map for the jewel on my way here!"

Arkon was shocked and quaked, "You lost what? How dare you lose something important like that! What are we supposed to do now? How will we find the guardians and the jewel without the map?"

Tynar answered, "I'm really sorry, my lord. I don't even know how that happened, but we can stay in this world until we find a way to find the map or the guardians. I came to this world specifically sixty years ago, and it changed very much. They are using something called money here; that thing is used for everything you need in this world."

Arkon replied, "I know what money is used for, idiot. Halinor told me. Now where can we get this money?"

"It's easy. Use your power to transform the stone into gold, and then we can sell it and earn a lot of money," Tynar replied.

Arkon stared angrily and barked, "Are you kidding me? I lost my powers when I came here. How shall I do that?"

Tynar replied, "We must keep looking for the gate because it will stay open until we finish the task, but its place will change to another place. It must be under the guardians' protection in a magical place."

"There is something wrong that happened when we arrived here."

They both walked to find something to help them, and then Tynar said, "I have an idea. Let's find the person who descended from the ancestry; they are born to help immortals in this world."

Arkon looked at him. He thought to hit him, but he said, "I think you left your mind in Meridian." Then he stated, "How can we find that person if we don't have the map?"

Tynar realized that he was uttering a lot of stupid things. "My king, I will leave you here for a few minutes to change these clothes." Arkon looked at him and realized that Tynar was almost naked and wearing a strange apron. Tynar continued, "My king, please sit down here, and I will come back soon, so don't talk to anyone here and don't command because they will think that you are mad." Arkon sat down and indicated for him to leave.

Arkon thought, *I have been in this world for a few days now, and I am still powerless.* In the meantime, a girl crossed in front of him, yelling into her phone.

"I told you someone stole from me. Where are you? Come here and help me!" She ended the call. Then she looked straight and saw someone staring at her. She froze; she couldn't believe that there was a human being carrying all this beauty. She stood in front of him and did nothing. Arkon, who was staring at her too, felt something very strange when he saw her. He didn't hesitate and stood. Then he walked toward her. Arya saw him walking toward her and wondered, *Is he coming toward me? Do I know him?*

He stood beside her and said, "Do you know me?" She didn't answer. So, he repeated, "Do you know me?" Arya was shocked; the words were gone.

Then she woke up and said, "Oh, I'm sorry; I didn't want to bother you. I thought you were someone else."

Tynar came and saw Arkon talking to the girl, so he rushed when he saw her. He knew her immediately, so he whispered in Arkon's ear about what happened when he arrived and how she fainted, and the apron was hers. Arya left them and said, "Excuse me."

Arkon said, "If you tell me your name and where you live, I will make Tynar pay you soon!" The girl turned to him and thought, *OMG, even someone like him can be crazy.*

She replied, "I think your family is worried about you now. Please go back safe." Then she turned on her way to leave.

Arkon yelled, "How dare you! I'm still talking. I didn't say leave yet!" She turned again, and her facial expressions changed.

"What do you want?"

"Not me. I'm asking, what do you want?" Arkon replied. Arya thought, *This guy is absolutely mad. I must keep up with him.* "Okay, I want cash!"

"What? Cash? What do you mean by that?"

Arya thought, *Oh god, this day will last forever.* She said, "Don't worry, please go home safely." Then she walked; he followed her and caught her hand! She looked at him and yelled, "What do you want? Leave my hand, or I will call the police."

In the meantime, her friend (the nurse) came because she had called him previously and heard her voice. He rushed and pushed Arkon's hand away from her and stated, "Are you okay?"

Arkon yelled and said, "How dare you, miserable human! Do you know who I am? I'm an immortal and the next king of the great world of Meridian!"

Both Arya and her friend Matt laughed. Arya giggled. "I knew that. Why are we stuck with mad people even out of work? Matt, let's go."

They both walked, but then Matt returned and gave him the clinic's business card and said, "Come and visit us at our clinic. Our doctor is brilliant." Then he followed Arya and left. Matt told Arya, "Do you know that you are destined to be a doctor! You meet the patients everywhere."

"Shut up and tell me where the nearest police station is!" she asked.

"Why? Come on. He's a madman."

"No, idiot, I'm not talking about the man. I want to tell them that someone stole my ring. I don't know who, but I think someone hit me on the head and took it because I don't remember what happened."

"Are you still drunk?" Matt asked.

"Go, you don't believe what I said. Go home." She went to the police station, and then she went home. She walked through a beautiful street where her home was located. There were yellow lights on the street on both sides, and the trees were high. She walked alone as if she were carrying the whole world's problems. She arrived at her home, and the main door was made from black iron in an old style. She entered and walked through the trees that were planted on both sides of the walking corner. It looked like these trees were old enough to carry ancient memories. The home was silent, not even like a cemetery, cold and pale. When she opened the door and entered, the floor was littered with books and stuff, as if ten people were living in this house. She opened the fridge and took an instant bowl of noodles to eat. It looked like this girl had suffered enough loneliness.

In the meantime, Arkon and his servant Tynar were searching for a place to stay, alone without money, lost in the humans' world.

The next morning, a sharp CEO of a resort, Julian, kicked off his busy day with morning briefings from his subordinates. He wasn't keen on attending a meeting with a bank that wanted his business but was told it would be suitable to comply.

Arya arrived at the clinic. Matt was cleaning the ground, when he said, "You should go to the bank and deal with the loan issue." She went to the bank, and the state of her finances were pretty bleak. The banking agent suggested refinancing at a much higher interest rate, which appeared to be her only option. So she kept waiting for her application to be approved for hours and was sidelined by her banker when CEO Julian walked in. Incensed, Arya marched over to the room and got even angrier when she heard the CEO being offered a fraction of the interest rate she has to pay.

She walked inside the room and talked angrily, "Excuse me, I was suffering and waiting for few hours, and you didn't tell me about the decision about my loan request, and why did you offer me a 7% interest, and I just heard that you offered this man a 1% interest? Why do you make a difference between your clients?"

The man, Julian, spoke. "Please help the lady first." Then he stood with his assistant and said, "My financial team will finish the process."

Then he walked to leave when the bank manager said, "Sir, you can't leave now; please stay."

The bank agent told Arya, "Give Mr. Julian an apology right now. He is leaving because you bothered him!"

Julian turned, put his hands behind him, walked to the agent, and conceded, "No, that is not why I'm leaving; because it's the bank's mistake to reveal the percentage of the interests to other clients, you should say your apology to the girl." Then he said to Arya, "I will talk to the bank in order to accept your loan request."

Arya replied, "And why would you do that for me?"

"It's obvious that you don't know how to accept good behavior." Then he left.

Outside the bank, Matt went from car to car, leaving business cards on windshields. He got upset to see one driver using the card to wipe away bird poop and protested on the man's face. Julian came out of the car—this was his driver—and Arya joined as well, wondering about the commotion.

Matt broke the car's windshield, insisting that the driver shouldn't remove the mess with their card. Julian's assistant took out their business card and gave it to Matt, and said, "We will call you to pay the broken windshield expenses." Then they rode the car silently.

At the river, where Arkon and Tynar spent their last night, Tynar came, and he was searching for the magical map. "My king, I kept searching for it, but I couldn't find it. I think I lost it on my way; that's mean we will not be able to find it," Tynar said.

"Then let's go and find the gate land; it's protected by the guardians. Maybe we can find the person that descended from the strain there. Now let's go to that place!"

At the clinic, Matt kicked himself for damaging the wiper, afraid of the exorbitant repair cost. Arya tried to get in touch with the real estate office, and when she couldn't, she decided to head over to another estate to deal with her land's sale, hoping that she would sell it for a good amount to help herself. Her car was old, and the GPS system wasn't working clearly. At the same time, Arkon and Tynar rode a farmer truck, heading out of the city to some land that Tynar suspected was the land of the magical gate.

The truck driver, who let them off on a rural road and pointed them in the direction of their destination, Arya met with the realtor, asked him to take some care to sell her pile of rocks, even if it required lowering the price. The realtor suggested halving the price, which made her exclaim in dismay.

The heir, Arkon, and his servant, Tynar, arrived at the bare plot of land. They found the land of the gate, but it was not crossable. Tynar said, "You can cross the gate only after you have got the Jewel of Meridian."

Arkon replied, "The humans can't see the gate even if they come here. I thought I would see the guardians or the person from the strain here."

"By the way, the person from the strain will not recognize us if we don't show the magical map!" Tynar said.

Arkon replied, "Don't worry; I have a plan for that case, and especially if the person we are looking for is a girl!"

"A girl? How did you know?" Tynar asked.

"Because Halinor told me that the person who descended from the strain is a girl!"

In the meantime, the sound of an old car came behind them. They turned, and Arya got out of the car and said, "Excuse me, what are you doing here? This is my land." Arkon couldn't turn to her because he saw something weird on one of the rocks when Arya approached them and stated, "Are you here to buy the land?" When Arkon turned, she took a minute to process. She thought, *What's he doing here?*

Arkon said, "Why shall I buy my land?"

Tynar rushed to them to prevent Arkon from saying anything. Arkon stared at Tynar and said, "I told you if we would come here, we would find the strain's girl, and it seems that destiny made us meet yesterday." Arya couldn't understand what he was talking about. She remembered what Matt told her about her destiny with the mad people.

Arkon walked over purposely to pour on his godly charm, running a finger along her face and saying in his gravest voice, "I have searched for you for ages. My servant. Meeting like this is a pleasure. Be moved by what pleases me." Arya slapped his hand away and hurried back to her car. She started to drive off just as Tynar jumped in front of her car to stop her, and he got knocked down.

Tynar assured her that he was fine, but Arkon declared that he wasn't, and Tynar got right back on the ground, feigning injury, which was how she ended up driving the two of them, offering to drop them off at a nearby hospital. Arkon declared that they were going with her and ordered her to 'awaken' and understand everything. Arya asked if Arkon was currently receiving any medical attention and almost offered her services before stopping herself. When she referred to Tynar as his friend, Arkon replied, "He is not a friend. He is my servant," not giving her any reason to change her misconception of him. *Is he crazy?*

Arkon observed the inner workings of the car closely, mostly ignoring her comments, while Arya followed the GPS's increasingly convoluted directions. The roads got rougher and rougher until they ended up in a dead end in the mountains, and in frustration, Arya rested her head on the steering wheel. Arkon offered to drive for her, but she declined and started to move back— right as the car ran out of gas. There was no cell service either, so she decided they would have to walk to get help. Arkon told her to rest since she was tired, offering Tynar instead. Arya pointed out that he was injured, and Tynar played up the hurt act…until Arkon declared that he was not, and Tynar was immediately better. Arya didn't argue too hard and handed over the cash and a gas container, sending poor Tynar off on his way.

Arya napped in the car while Arkon waited outside, and after some time passed, she woke and suggested Arkon rest inside the car too. He balked at her calling him 'Hey there', and he informed her that his name is Arkon, listing off all his heavenly credentials again. This time, he added, "And also your master."

Arya sighed to herself. *I keep forgetting he's a patient.* In psychiatrist mode, she asked why he thinks he's an immortal, and he retorted, "Then why do you think you are human?" Point taken. She revised her question to ask what an immortal is.

"As a human, is it teaching you to wish to receive?" he asked. "You appear to wish to converse about the ultimate essence of the world." He informed her that the water, sky, and land immortals are nature and that he is therefore nature.

Puzzled, Arya asked if he was calling himself a natural person. "I am nature," he repeated. "And among those, the nature of natures." That did nothing to clarify anything for her.

In the car, she stole glances at him, wondering how he looked so normal when he was clearly not. She asked if he has family, and he replied that perhaps yes, perhaps no. "In the immortals' realm, we do not have family relations that you humans think of." Then he called her servant, and she automatically responded before even thinking about it.

Arkon asked if what she really needed most is money and why, and she replied that money allows you to be happy. He told her he was asking because he thinks he can do that for her.

For a moment, she seemed to take him at his word until he added that he couldn't give her money right now because of his circumstances. Arya chided herself for believing him.

Arkon added, "But if what you need the most is money, because money makes you happy, then what you need the most is happiness." That's close enough to hit home, though he added, "But I have no interest in the happiness of a human woman, so I will repay you with money!"

Arya suggested they go for help, but it wasn't long before they realized they didn't know the way down. She suggested heading back, and while he agreed with the sentiment, he balked again because she called him 'Hey there'.

Arkon told her sternly, "For the last time, listen up. I am not 'Hey there', but Arkon. The next king of Meridian and the next emperor of the immortals' realm."

Arya glared, then retorted that her name is Arya, not 'Servant'. She insisted that he should be addressing her adequately, and he just noted, "You are quite rude."

In the meantime, Arya spotted a wild boar nearby, and she grabbed Arkon's wrist and urged him to run. The boar chased them down the road, gaining on them as they ran.

Arkon looked over at Arya, then pulled her hand from his wrist and grabbed her hand properly, taking the lead. They were very nearly back at the car when Arya fumbled with the keys, dropping them on the road. With the boar gaining on them, she yelled for him to head for the opened trunk. With seconds to spare, they climbed into the trunk and closed the door.

The boar slammed into the car multiple times, rocking it back and forth. It seemed to give up and leave, but when Arya lifted the lid to check, the boar actually looked at her and slammed itself into the car again.

Arya screamed in fear while Arkon cradled her protectively, and with every slam of the car, she grew increasingly panicked. After several long minutes, finally, a bang sounded, and the vehicle stopped shaking. The trunk lid lifted, revealing Tynar, who explained that he ran into a hunter who chased the boar into the woods.

Arya was rattled enough that she let Arkon drive them back and remarked that she thought he didn't know how to drive. He informed her that this was his first time and that he found it quite fun.

Arya insisted that he pull over, but he ordered her to rest, saying, "I am extending to you a show of grace, so do not refuse. Doing this for you is naturally an immortal's duty and generosity."

She ordered him to pull the car over, so naturally, he floored it.

When he finally did pull over, she ran to the sidewalk to dry-heave. She took her car keys from him, curtly thanked him for his help today, and walked away. Arkon called after her to inform her of the ancient agreement between her ancestors and the immortals to serve them for all future generations. "It does not matter that you did not make the promise," he said. "If the immortals wish it, you, the descendant of servants, must honor your family's promise and serve me." With that, he ordered her to take him to her home!

Arya said that she'd take him to a hospital, and he replied that her refusal would only make things harder for her. "Things are plenty hard enough already, so I don't care," she stated.

And added, "You're right—what I really need is maybe happiness. Because I truly am exhausted. So please, leave now. I ask this favor."

As she walked away again, Arkon called her dim for not awakening despite his attempt to teach her. "It can't be helped," he told Tynar.

"As you said, I was trying my best not to use the last resort. But I'll have to use it."

As Tynar sputtered something about what that means for his powers, Arkon yelled after Arya, who turned back. He walked up to her and said, "This is the grace of my highness, so be awakened." And then he kissed her.

Chapter Three
It Resumes

In Meridian, Queen Wera, the great queen of the immortals' world, sat on her throne. Suddenly, she felt a rough heartbeat; she looked up to the diamond ceiling and felt the jewel's beat through the universe. She left the great hall, running out to the magical lake, a magical water reflecting what was happening with anyone you asked for. She talked and said, "Show me Prince Arkon."

The watercolor changed and started to shape the vision. The queen saw him kissing a girl; she gazed at the girl's neck and saw the necklace. The queen was shocked; she sat on the lake's edge, and then she spoke. "It's true! The prophecy is true." And a smile drew from her mouth.

Back on earth, Arya was surprised, but her eyes fluttered close while his stayed open, and he seemed flustered by that. He pushed her back and stammered that she was now his person. He thought that kissing her would let her know the memories of her family and that she is from a strain that serves the immortals.

He waited expectantly for Arya's gratitude, although she just blinked at him uncomprehendingly. His servant Tynar hurried over to pick Arkon up and remove him from the situation. A safe distance away, Tynar put Arkon down, who was indignant at this treatment. A second later, Arya's scream cut through the air: "You are a crazy bastard!"

Tynar fretted that the information awakening didn't happen. Arkon ordered him to fix the situation with Arya, and when Tynar hesitated, he figured that he'll do it himself. Tynar protested, though, and told him that he can't go around kissing human women suddenly and that he'll get slapped if he goes to her now.

Arya returned home all flustered and upset, although it was as much with herself as it was with Arkon. "Why did you close your eyes?" she wailed, mortified. "I have to find a logical reason for closing my eyes."

She told herself to confront the issue and overcome it, only to hear Arkon's voice calling, "Hey, Servant!" She turned to see Arkon in her mirror, and the moment of the kiss replayed before her eyes. She yelled at the couple onscreen not to do it and heard his voice saying that something should be entering her heart and mind, just as a bell rang from afar.

Arya denied it emphatically and envisioned going to that far-off bell to silence it. She ordered Arkon's image to leave, and to her relief, the mirror returned to normal.

At his floating house near the river, Arkon thought of Tynar's warning that he'd get slapped for kissing Arya. He called Arya quite stupid for not recognizing an immortal's grace for what it is. He looked over at a snoring Tynar in the belief that Arya would awaken and seek him out.

Then he thought about his initial flustered reaction to the kiss and told himself, "It's nothing. It's just that the world has changed."

The next morning, Arya groggily got up, and her first thought was last night's kiss. Then she saw how late it was and panicked until her alarm clock rang and reminded her that it was Sunday. Was that nurse Matt's voice blaring? The alarm rang again to warn her not to go back to sleep and to go exercise instead.

It rang with more nagging instructions. Arya yanked out the batteries and vowed to kill Matt and go to hell. She tried to go back to sleep, but it was useless by now.

At the park, by the river, Arkon wondered why there were so many humans there today and got shooed off the walking path by a cadre of power-walking women. He was intrigued by the workings of a bicycle, and Tynar suggested he check out the skate park, where a competition was underway.

Arkon was not impressed by the skateboarders' tricks, though he did observe their movements closely. Tynar whined at Arkon to give it a try for the prize money, so when the announcer assumed Arkon was a contestant, Arkon confirmed that all he had to do were all four tricks to win the cash. He even declared that he'd win second and third place too, and he picked up a skateboard lying nearby.

Arya happened by, out for some exercise after all, just as Arkon made his way to the top of a ramp. He let loose, hitting several complicated tricks on various apparatus while the crowd went wild. As he flew through the air, he locked eyes with Arya, and she heard his words again about something entering her heart and mind.

He called out, "You're here," as he passed, and Arya hurried away. Only moments later, his voice called out, "You in front, Servant! I am here."

He was skateboarding after her, and Arya hastened her pace. Arya wondered why she was running away just as Tynar asked the same thing, only to have Arkon declare, "She's not running away. She's seeking me out."

He shouted out to Arya that he was here, calling her stupid as though she were running away not having seen him.

Arya darted into a tunnel, but when Arkon got there, all he saw was a group of women doing yoga, all wearing giant sun visors and face masks. It was a perfect cover for Arya, who blended into the crowd. The women started power walking, and Arkon couldn't quite make out where Arya was.

It allowed Arya to escape, and later she broke off from the pack, and she caught her breath by the waterside. A soccer ball flew by and landed in the water, and as she looked out at the river, her hand started to shake, and she was overcome with a feeling of pain.

It prompted a flashback to a younger Arya struggling underwater, begging for someone to save her. She cried for her father and sank further down.

Arkon and Tynar returned to their floaty house by the river, gloomed because the contest refused to give them their prize, thinking Arkon was an expert trying to score an easy buck. Tynar whined that he'd told Arkon not to go all-out with his skills and that if he had those powers, he'd use them for Arkon's sake.

Arkon said, "I was going to win all those prizes for you, Tynar!" That made Tynar overcome with gratitude. Until Arkon added, "…Is not something you expected I would say, is it?"

Tynar slumped down, feeling dejected and hungry, and told Arkon, "My lord, I think you should give up with the human servant awakening."

Arkon declared that they would be going 'home' now and handed over Matt's business card.

In the meantime, resort CEO Julian was told that there was some resistance with a piece of land they were trying to buy, which belongs to a certain chairman, Harold Hale. Julian said he'd deal with it.

Julian's secretary heard that it'd take some time to acquire the part to fix his windshield wiper, which made Julian think of Arya and how the bill would be pretty high.

Matt was deflated to hear the repair amount and broached the topic cautiously with Arya, wondering if he could find a way to lessen the price. Arya told him to stand tall and handle it through insurance. Matt updated her on a couple of patients, and Arya heaved a tired sigh, which seemed to echo in the room, though she didn't see anything there. The door opened. Matt entered and said, "Did you know that the building owner sent his agent? And he told me that they want to raise the deposit because we are delayed in paying the rent." Arya stood, and she was surprised.

"What? Oh my god, what is happening with us!" Then she rushed out to see the building owner.

She came running around the bend just as Arkon stepped out of another cab. At the same time, Julian's car stopped at the red light, and an elderly man walked across the long crosswalk and declined multiple offers from pedestrians to help him across the way. Arya jogged ahead of the man, but then—to the surprise of both Arkon and Julian—she pulled out a phone and pretended to read it, slowing her walk to keep pace with the old man. Essentially, she was shielding him from impatient drivers who started honking when the light changed, and he was still walking. Julian smiled to himself, and his driver noted that she was suited to her doctor's gown. Arya lost sight of her landlord and jumped when Arkon appeared in front of her. Assuming she had been awakened, he informed her that she wouldn't have to provide much help while he was here—merely a house to stay in, food for them, clothes to wear, and a lot of money!

Arya pulled Tynar aside to speak to him as the patient's guardian, advising him to take Arkon to the hospital. When Tynar said they have nowhere to go, she told him to try social services, stating that it's the state's responsibility to help them, not hers.

As she speaks, she remembers.

FLASHBACK – ARYA'S CHILDHOOD

Arya came back home, and the living room was overrun with other children eating at her table and playing with toys. She tossed aside her bag angrily. She headed to her room and started crying.

END FLASHBACK

Arkon asked, "Why did you help the old man a minute ago if you don't care to help the others?"

"A man! I didn't help anyone. You are wrong." He didn't believe her and noted that she was not honest. Arya told them not to show up again, threatening to call the police the next time. Arkon warned that if she goes now, he'll abandon her for good. "That's the best thing I've heard," she stated, then walked away.

Arya received a call from Matt, who told her she needed to sign paperwork for her old patient who was admitting himself into the hospital. When he paused, another voice whispered, "You're in trouble—do you know who that is?" It wasn't Matt, but another voice added, "You'll be in agony." She whirled angrily, thinking it was Arkon, but found nobody there!

In an underground parking lot, a car screeched to a stop just in front of Julian, and a young woman stepped out, sniping at Julian for coming here to mooch some more. Julian just ignored her, turning instead to the older man who stepped out: Chairman Hale, who warmly greeted Julian as a nephew. The snippy woman is the chairman's granddaughter, Miranda, who snapped that Julian isn't family just because he's in the family registry! It was Miranda who seemed to be the money-sucking leech here, and she whined for her grandpa to give her an entertainment company so she could pursue being a star. Grandpa refused, leaving her pouting.

Inside the elevator with Julian, Chairman Hale sighed that he had spent a lot of money sending Miranda to medical school. He seemed a scrooge type of miser and happily picked up a coin from the floor. Chairman Hale asked about Julian's plan to build a new resort and cut to the chase. "How much will I make from the deal?"

Meanwhile, Arya tried to make her case to her landlord's agent, asking him to talk to his boss about not raising the deposit at the clinic. He relayed his boss's sentiments on the matter: that she should move to another building since she can't even pay the rent here. Arya said she'd talk to the chairman herself, but the agent barked that she couldn't.

Julian discussed the plan for his resort, but a knock interrupted their conversation. He sat up with interest when Arya walked in, and she was a bit abashed to recognize him before making her case about the increased deposit. Chairman Hale laid out his stance clearly and simply: pay up or move out.

Left with no recourse, Arya bowed and exited. As she waited for the elevator, she heard Arkon's words from the other night: that she is his person now and will encounter all sorts of troubles if she doesn't accept it. She wondered if this kind of trouble was what he meant before shaking aside the thought—and then a voice rang out, "Please give me water! I'm so thirsty!"

Arya looked around, confused, and her eyes landed on a withering plant. The voice added, "Give me water! Will you have me dry out and die?" Then she bumped into another woman and could actually hear her thoughts as the other woman griped internally at her for blocking her path.

Julian joined her at the elevator and suggested that she try the bank again. She told him it was none of his business, asking why he was such a busybody. He replied that she is as well, reminding her of her actions at the crosswalk.

She was embarrassed that he saw that and said she was just walking. He noted that she couldn't be honest about it, echoing Arkon's words, though he added that it was not a criticism. When he mentioned the wiper repair, Arya cut him off to say she'll let insurance handle it, and Julian said, "I was going to say you don't have to pay for it. Is that being a busybody?" Arya practically kicked herself but forced herself to agree to pay him back.

Arya heard that her former patient ran away before being admitted to the psychiatric hospital as planned. Still, she argued that he was no longer her responsibility and told Matt to let the hospital handle the situation.

In the meantime, Arkon and Tynar rode the subway, and when a stomach grumbled, this time it seemed to come from Arkon. He stared longingly at a child eating a hotdog, though he haughtily denied it and refused Tynar's offer of his remaining cupcake.

Arkon caught a glimpse of his neighbor's phone screen, and his eyes widen. He could only see the back of a woman's head in the video, but he wondered, *Cornelia?*

He followed the woman off the subway at the next stop, and Tynar noticed too late to join him. The subway train departed with Tynar still in it, leaving Arkon stranded alone on the platform. He looked up across the way at the opposite side, where Arya's patient was standing. The two men locked eyes, and the patient saw the air rippling in between them, like water.

It was not long before Arya's patient posted the encounter on his Instagram account. And Matt called Arya to tell her that the patient talked about having met an immortal on the subway platform. She just sighed that she was the one who'd like to meet a real immortal right now.

Arkon returned to his floaty house, accompanied by Arya's patient, who bought him an array of food. Arkon did his best to keep his nose in the air and ignore the food. Although the craving grew stronger and became increasingly difficult for him to resist, he tried to resist the human instinct of hunger.

Arya's patient snapped a selfie with Arkon in the background, saying that people will believe him now that he has proof, and uploaded it on his Instagram. He chattered on about another believer friend whom he called TF1004 and apologized for not having met Trump yet. Arkon asked blankly, "Who's Trump?"

Arya arrived at the subway platform just as Matt informed her of a new Instagram post. He sent it to her, adding that this patient attempted suicide the last time he was in a mental hospital. That news made her take this situation more seriously, but she still insisted that they should leave it to the others.

Exhausted, she slumped onto a bench and asked aloud, "Why does everyone do this to me? I won't live like this." She took a reluctant look at the Instagram post and recognized Arkon in the background. Matt texted her the location of the picture, probably knowing she'll end up going despite all the protests. Arya's patient was shocked that Arkon had no idea who Trump was and started rattling off facts about his life and career. Arkon said dismissively that none of that made any sense to him and that the only thing he can say with certainty is that this Trump person isn't going to save the world.

Arya spotted them and hid her face behind a newspaper while the stunned patient asked who would save the world if not Trump? Arkon said he doesn't care about human matters, and when the patient mentioned TF1004, Arkon stated, "He's a fake."

That crushed the patient, who yelled that he was lying. Arkon stared him in the eye and started his own list of credentials as an immortal, emperor of the immortals' realm, and said, "One person can ruin the world, but one person can't save it. And so, that is not something Trump can do. So do your work properly instead of wandering around like this."

Arya worried that Arkon was handling this badly, and the patient yelled in frustration that he couldn't do anything no matter how hard he tried and that he can't live like this. Arya called out to the patient and urged him to talk to her, promising to listen to what he really wants to say—that he wanted to show his father, and that's why he's been trying to meet Trump. He screamed that he had already tried to talk to her, but she ignored him.

The patient refused to let Arya near and told himself that he'd just talk to TF1004, the only person who listened to him. He started walking toward the water, and Arya's legs froze, unable to get any closer. It was her trauma, triggered, and she whispered, "Dad?" Arya told Arkon to grab the patient, but he told her to do it herself. Unable to move, Arya tried to appeal to him with words, but he accused her of pretending to listen to him while never intending to save him at all. She denied it, but the sight of the water made her shrink back, and Arya noticed her breathing growing ragged.

FLASHBACK – 14 YEARS AGO

In her high school uniform, Arya stood on the bridge, trying to call her father, who wouldn't pick up the phone. She broke down crying, then said, "I will make you regret it for the rest of your life." Arya flogged her cell phone into the water, then got up onto the railing of the bridge. She hit the water and sank down into its depths, but as she looked up toward the surface, she thought, *Save me.* She started to kick and swim upward, but she didn't gain any ground, and her cries grew more desperate as she sobbed for her father. Her limbs went slack.

"I regretted it," Arya said. Then she added, "It was cold and dark, and scary, and nobody was there."

But somehow, teenage Arya made it to the riverbank and pulled herself up out of the water.

The patient said that he was going to die, accusing her of not believing that he'd do it. He jumped into the river and immediately started flailing, and Arya dropped her phone in her panic, feeling helpless. She prayed for someone to save him, thinking of her father again, and tried to force herself closer to the water's edge.

He sank deeper into the water, and his body eventually went limp. Arkon watched as Arya forced herself to run toward the river and then grabbed her as she ran past, calling her rash and complaining of how noisy she was being. He solemnly entrusted his chicken drumstick to her, then dove in. The fear overcame her, and Arya sank to the ground, begging for him to come back. She broke down into a mess of guilt and fear, huddled low.

Moments later, Arkon reappeared to remind her that she was noisy. He was dripping wet, with the patient sprawled out on the grass nearby. Arya hurried to perform CPR on him, starting with chest compressions and moving on to mouth-to-mouth. Just before she made contact, he sputtered and woke, insisting he was saving his lips for the immortals.

Arya hugged her patient, apologizing and thanking him. Arkon was pretty nonchalant about the whole thing until he spotted his precious drumstick lying in the dirt, and then he screamed at her, "I told you to take care of this! I'm not saying I'm going to eat it, but my Tynar would be hungry!"

Arkon looked uneasy when Arya started to approach and backed up nervously as she got close. But then she grabbed him around the waist and held on tight, thanking him too. It threw him for a loop, and as he stood there stunned, the queen's voice said, "Fate…is fate."

In Meridian, the queen's maid asked, "Your Majesty, what do you mean by fate?"

She answered, "He won't tell her, but she keeps pestering for an answer." Then she added firmly, "It is a secret of nature."

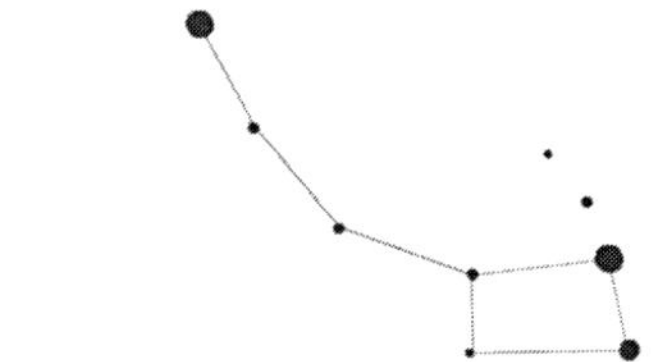

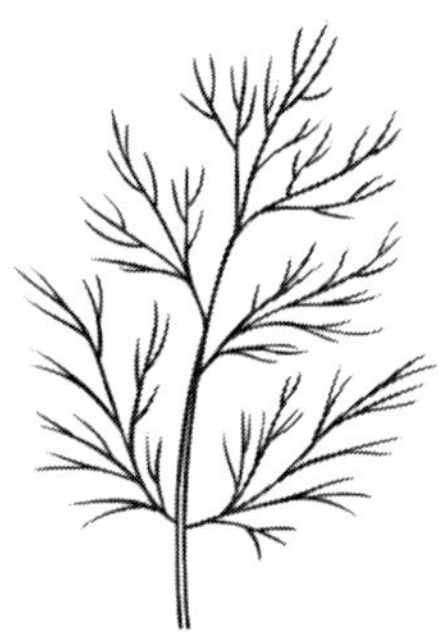

Chapter Four
Devotion

After Arkon dived into the river to rescue the suicidal patient, an ambulance arrived to take the patient away. Arya remained behind with Arkon and asked hesitantly, "Is that floatie house where you are staying? And where is Tynar? Are you okay?"

He stared at her and said, "Yes."

Then Arya stated, "You can't stay here!"

He immediately responded, "Are you finally deciding to give me your home and yourself!"

"Me? No, of course not."

"So why did you say that? What did you mean?"

"I think you need to go and ask for a government institution's help."

He turned on his back and said, "I don't understand that. If you wouldn't do that, then leave!"

She poorly replied, "Okay, then I hope you will be fine; thank you again; goodbye."

As Arya turned to go, a voice said disapprovingly, "You don't recognize kindness!" She looked around wonderingly, and when she continued walking again, that voice barked, "You ungrateful thing!" And a third time: "You with no conscience!" The voices only got more persistent after that, and some days later, Arya called her friend for advice, sporting serious dark circles as she recounted the voices coming from things like flowers, ants, and water. When Arya stepped on a leaf, she heard a yelp of pain, and the cactus on her desk accused her of cruelty for withholding water. Initially assuming she was just tired, the more voices she heard, the more she found she couldn't write it off as plain fatigue.

She consulted a med school friend, Nani, for advice about the hearing problem. Nani ran through the symptoms and ruled out certain conditions, suggesting that perhaps the answer lied with the first voices she heard that called her ungrateful. In other words, maybe it was her guilty conscience for ignoring someone in need of help.

Arya protested that it doesn't make sense for a guilty conscience to result in auditory hallucinations, but Nani described it as being quite tender-hearted but overcompensating by acting the opposite because she disliked that about herself. As she described the patient, Arya's mind flashed to recent incidents, like helping a grandpa cross the street and how both Arkon and CEO Julian noted that she couldn't be honest about her reasons.

Nani supposed that Arya's behavior was rooted in some past trauma and pointed out that she ignored Arkon even after hearing that his friend had abandoned him and really needed help.

Arkon was back with Tynar at the park, and they pondered a cell phone and how Arkon could have seen Cornelia inside of it. In concern, Tynar wondered how they'd free her from the tiny rectangle prison and whispered to the phone, "My lady, Cornelia! Can you hear me!" For once, Arkon seemed to know more about humans than Tynar, and he started to explain how phones work. Unfortunately, that was when a skateboarding kid nearby demanded his phone back. Arkon handed it over, but the kid had to yank it out of his clenched fingers.

The kid asked them, "Why don't you have a cell phone, and are you both adults?"

Arkon inquired, "Where can we get this device?"

That landed them in a mobile store, but they quickly realized they didn't understand any of the terms and, moreover, had no money.

Tynar headed off to work on a part-time job, leaving hungry Arkon with puffed rice snacks and water to fill his stomach. Feeling belittled and angry, Arkon winded up to throw the snacks into the river…but pulled back at the last second, unable to do it. After days of this, Arya finally appeared at the park, her dark circles deep and her face haggard. She started to say that she hadn't been as diligent as she should have been as a doctor, just as her ankle rolled and she stumbled. Arkon grabbed her hand, and she seemed to feel a moment between them.

Then he told her, "I've thought of nothing but you all the time. There where the sun rises in the east until the sun sets in the west, I have only thought of you. No matter how I tried, I could not break free from thoughts of you."

A little flustered then, Arya asked, "Why?"

He replied, "I could not understand how you could be so foolish and dim-witted, and because I could not comprehend for the life of me, I could not help but keep thinking of you."

Arya replied, "I really pity you, and I really want to help you. I recommend you my professor for psychiatric help, who is much more skilled and helpful than me."

Arkon replied, "If there's one thing I learned here, it's that speaking the truth makes people think of him as abnormal—just as you would seem if you admitted to being an immortal's servant." He denied that was the case, but he pointed out, "I am the only one who believes you. Is it an easy thing to earn someone's faith? How remarkable is it to have someone who fully believes in me?" His words unsettled Arya, who walked away, telling herself she had done as much as she could. Then Arkon reminded her of his earlier words: that if she didn't accept him, she would encounter all sorts of incidents!

Arya returned to her office a nervous wreck, muttering to herself over and over that she felt positively light and refreshed. Her cactus clamored for attention, complaining about her poor treatment, and Arya increased the volume of her self-affirmation. Matt entered her room because he heard her screaming. He yelled, "What's happened? What's wrong?"

She stared at him in a creepy, weird way and said, "You should knock on the door before you enter."

The nurse replied, "Doctor, why are you so strict these days? Why are you always yelling at me? You should take a rest and sleep more. What are you doing at night rather than sleeping?" She sat on her chair, saying nothing. Then she gave him a sign to get out.

Arya called her friend Nani for more advice, this time about a man. Nani asked if he was good-looking, and Arya blurted, "Yes," before catching herself. She explained that there was a man who spouted off these ominous sayings, like those monks in horror dramas, who warned of bad omens that you know shouldn't be ignored. She asked if that could happen in real life, then cut herself off to say, of course not, and hung up before Nani could even reply.

Arya's phone rang; she saw that Matt was calling her. She answered, "What do you want? Why are you calling? It's three meters between our offices."

"I'm in front of your door, but I'm afraid of you, so I will tell you what I have from here! I booked all the appointments for Thursday, and I have news for you."

"What?" she asked.

"Do you want the bad news first or the good one?" Matt asked.

"Say what you have."

"Well, the police called, and there is nothing new about the diamond thief, and also, the bank agent called and told me that they rejected your loan request. Finally, the building owner decided that he would not force us to leave, but he asked for a higher rent."

She asked, "What about the good news?"

He answered, "I just told you they would not force us to leave as long as we pay a higher rent." She hung up, closed her fist with anger, and got out of her office. She saw Matt in front of the door carrying an envelope!

"What is that?" she asked.

"This may be the last solution for our problems. It happens today!"

"What is this?"

"It's an invitation to a fundraising event for your medical school alumni." He suggested that she go and rub elbows there, which she rejected flat out.

She couldn't even think about that because most of her friends found themselves in good places in their careers. So she felt that she couldn't show up, and she looked less than them, but she was confused because this was not the proper time for pride and dignity, and she was on the edge of bankruptcy. While Matt was talking and she was not listening to him at all, she rethought about going to the party without telling him, but her thoughts were not clear enough to make the final decision.

In the meantime, Tynar came in a hurry to see Arkon, who was sitting in the park, and said, "My lord, I saw a massive amount of gold, a huge place built from the gold. If we cut a small piece, no one would notice." Tynar guided him to a huge building that was reflecting the sunlight.

Arkon stared at him and said, "We were here many times, and you didn't know what that is. When I saw it for the first time, I thought that the humans really loved gold, but then I realized that this was glass and it was only reflecting the sunlight."

"No way; that really looks like gold," Tynar replied. Arkon turned and walked away. Then he caught a glimpse of the screen mounted on the building, featuring Cornelia's commercial. He called Tynar's attention to it, but by the time he pointed up at the building, the ad had changed, and Cornelia was gone.

At night, Arya ended up heading to that fundraiser after all, struggling in her painful heels to climb the steep hill to the fancy hotel. She sat on the curb to rest her aching feet, just as a car pulled over; it was Julian, on his way to that very same hotel. Her pride asserted itself before her sense could, declining a ride. She immediately regretted it, but Julian accepted her word and left before she could take it back. She called her friend, Nani, and asked her if she would attend the party. Her friend said, "No, I'm not coming because everyone will treat me as a stranger. Also, I don't need money."

Arya replied, "Actually, I'm going because I need money."

Nani replied, "How much do you need? I can lend you some money."

"No, thank you. I already have a lot of debts. I'll go now; talk to you later."

At the hotel, Julian's secretary suggested that sometimes people say the opposite of what they mean and that they're really asking for help when they decline it. Julian was startled to consider that Arya may have wanted his help after all, but he shook off the thought, certain that she was very clear about what she wanted.

Arkon and Tynar went to Arya's clinic because Arkon was convinced that his speech earlier about believing in her got through to Arya. He arrived with Tynar and found the clinic empty. A woman who owned a grocery shop next to the clinic told Arkon that the clinic was closed today because the doctor went to the party at the Grand Park Hotel. Tynar asked, "Shall we come back tomorrow?"

Arkon answered, "Let's go." They rode a taxi and gave him the address of the hotel that the woman told them about.

In the meantime, Arya didn't fit in with her snooty classmates who greeted her, practically snickering at the idea that her clinic was struggling. A flower bouquet distracted Arya by talking at her. Arya was avoiding the plants recently because she always heard their voices. She asked her classmate, "Why did you bring flowers?"

Her mate answered, "There is one of the old students who supports the hospital, so my manager asked me to present it to him." Arya thought that this person could be the solution that she was looking for.

Then she asked, "Who is he?" Then her mate pointed at the man. When Arya looked at him, she was shocked because it was Julian. Arya couldn't believe how her luck has left her these days. Her classmate waxed poetic about all of Julian's merits, but Arya retorted that he was very different on the inside. Julian was behind her and listened to what she said, and he joined the conversation. He made a friendly greeting for Arya and made it seem like they were quite cozy. He made their friends think that they were friends so that she could talk behind his back freely. Arya blushed and said, "I will go now; excuse me." She walked, and Julian followed her. She noticed him and said, "What was that? Are you trying to be the savior knight?"

He replied, "I didn't know that you were a student at my college."

"And what would you do if you knew? Would you lend me money?" Arya said. And she was shocked at what she had just said. Then she continued, "I'm sorry; I'm exhausted and don't know what I'm saying." In the meantime, a noise came from the entrance, and the people gathered because Miranda had arrived, the aspiring celebrity and Julian's snotty niece. When Arya saw her, she excused herself, saying, "There's someone it'll be tiring to run into."

Then Julian replied, "Me too. I don't want to stay here. See you later."

Then Arya walked to get out of the place because she didn't want to get involved with the noisy Miranda, but Miranda noticed her, followed her, and called out to her, forcing her to stop and acknowledge her. As Arya turned, she heard voices tittering from Miranda's flower bouquet, which repeated every snipe Miranda threw at her. Miranda crowed that Arya was the 'Three-Minute Goddess', a nickname she invented that meant that she looked like a goddess at first sight, but after three seconds, she turned into a beggar. Julian watched from across the room as Miranda made digs at Arya about being jealous of her. Arya calmly said, "Oh, Miranda, you never change. You are still that loser girl that tries to make herself look like a successful human being." She approached her and put her hand on Miranda's shoulder, and said, "Don't act like that; take care."

Miranda felt great anger. Then she said in a loud voice to let everyone hear, "Has your father not come back yet?"

Miranda told the crowd that Arya's father had gone to Africa on volunteer work and didn't return, calling him a great man who took in beggars and clothed and fed them. Somehow Miranda made those sound like bad things. Your father was so outstanding that he traded his own family's harmony for his greater love of humanity. Arya finally whirled with blazing eyes and raised a hand at Miranda, and then she snatched the roses out of her hands and screamed, "You be quiet!" The room quieted, and Arya became the focus of attention. She turned to leave quietly, but when Miranda grabbed at her, she ripped Arya's sleeve.

Arya stared at her and barked, "Are you done? Let me talk now. I know that doing good is stupid these days because of some people like you. But you fool, even if you don't like it, you should fake it because of the people around you. I always knew that you were just a fake and stupid girl, but I didn't think that you would be like this. I really pity you." Then Arya got out of the place, and she was dizzy. Then Miranda followed her. She was screaming after her.

Outside the hotel, she tried to follow Arya, but Arkon, who had just arrived, blocked her path and said, "Why are you following my woman to harass her!"

Arya turned back, surprised at his interference, while Arkon explained that she was affiliated with him and that Miranda needed his permission to harass her. Then Miranda got recognized by other visitors and stomped off in a hurry.

Arya looked defeated when Arkon joined her, and she cried as she said, "The flowers were driving me crazy with their chatter." Arkon took in Arya's ripped sleeve and the tears running down her face. He shrugged off his suit jacket and placed it over her shoulders and reminded her of his warning.

Arkon hailed a taxi and opened the door for Arya. She got in. Then Julian and his driver crossed beside them and noticed what happened. On the drive home, Arya thought back to years ago when her father had ridden away in a taxi, and she had raced out of the house after the car. She thought now that she hadn't run after the car to hold back her father—it was to gather all her pain and find the strength to keep on living. That was the night she'd ended up at the bridge, knowing that her father would continue to do his work and that she would have to make her own way. *That night, I felt all of the pain in my body carved deep*, she thought. *And it was all because of my father. I decided to use that hate and resentment to live on. I ran to let my father go. It wasn't the last resort.*

The cab drove past that spot on the bridge in the present, and she looked out the window to see her teenage self there, crying by the railing.

They ended up by the river again, and when Arya asked why, Arkon replied that he didn't know where her house was, so he took her to his. She returned his jacket and thanked him, but he balked at her repeated instances of accepting his help and then left, accusing her of running off the minute she scored something.

They made Arya buy them a cell phone. Tynar said, "I promise you I will work and give you the money." Then he left for his part-time job. Arkon walked with Arya and explained to her how he saw someone he knew on one of these cell phones. Arya told him that that was an advertisement shown on the screens. Then she said, "I hope if you really were an immortal with magical powers, I would ask you for many wishes." In the meantime, Arkon was staring at one of the screens of the high building, and suddenly, the woman that he saw previously showed on the screen. He said, "Look, there she is, the woman that I'm looking for, Cornelia…"

Arya looked at him and said, "Oh my god, I'm sure now that you are crazy. This woman is one of the most famous actresses in the country. How could you even think of meeting her?"

Arkon replied, "If you can take me to the palace where Cornelia lives, I will be thankful to you, and I will leave you to live in peace." Arya thought it was the right opportunity to get rid of him and move on in her life.

The next morning, Arya took him to the luxurious resort that Cornelia lived in. She didn't know what she was doing, but she thought she could leave the illusion and all the whispers that she heard if he would finally leave her. He got out of the car and told Arya, "Thank you. I will give you every wish you wished for when I regain my powers again. Now you can leave. I will enter the palace alone." Then he left.

Arya wanted to move, but she couldn't because that wasn't a palace, and it wasn't Cornelia's house. It was a resort. She thought, *How can I leave him alone here when he knows nothing?* In the meantime, Julian's driver noticed the car stopped in front of the building with curiosity, and as they passed, he and Julian recognized Arya sitting inside. Julian stopped to ask what Arya was doing parked in front of his hotel, and she was startled to realize that he, of course, owned this place. She asked hesitantly if the actress Cornelia might be inside, and Julian replied that Cornelia was the brand model for his resort.

Meanwhile, Arkon was inside; he thought that this place was Cornelia's and all the workers there were her servants. He was also pleased with the way the hotel employees all bowed and thought that Cornelia had taught her staff well. He felt that she was near; he went off in search of her.

When he got out to the pool, he finally saw Cornelia, who was being prepped for a photoshoot by the pool. She heard Arkon calling out her name and looked up to see him standing there, smiling at her across the way. Arya rushed inside when she knew that Cornelia was inside because she knew that something bad would happen. When she entered, she saw Arkon fighting with the bodyguards. Then she ran to him, trying to stop him. She tried to break up the struggle, saying that he was her patient. At that, Cornelia's eyes opened, and she looked over at them sharply, watching as Arya got shoved to the ground in the scuffle. Arkon grew very angry to see that, and he grabbed the offending security guard and warned him to get away from his servant.

He kneeled to assist Arya and checked if she was okay, and an incensed Cornelia shouted, "Stop!" She strutted over to them, clocked that Arkon was holding Arya's wrist, and then delivered a slap to his face.

Arkon and Cornelia glared at each other for a long moment, and then Arya's voice cut in as she barked, "What are you doing?"

Cornelia asked, "Who is she?" Arya stepped in front of Arkon and declared herself as his guardian.

"I hit him because he did something deserving of being hit," Cornelia said.

That logic didn't work on Arya, who told Cornelia that people may call her a beauty goddess but that she let the praise go to her head. "Flowers wither," she said. "You think it'll last forever, don't you? No, it won't. Don't be shocked later when you shrivel up, and take care of your mental state in advance."

With that, Arya put her business card in Cornelia's hand and offered a celebrity discount. Grabbing Arkon's arm, she pulled him away. Arya thought that Cornelia didn't know Arkon and thought he was a madman, but the truth was the opposite. Arya was concerned; she felt responsible for Arkon. She still thought that he was sick and needed mental therapy.

At the car, Arkon chided Arya for stepping in, telling her that she erred and that Cornelia is, in fact, a real immortal who will never age or wither.

"I said I was your guardian. For the first time, I wanted to take you out of your world using my methods. But I see you have no desire to leave it."

Arkon said that their worlds were different. So she asked again if he really needed to meet an immortal. He nodded, so she called her friend Nani.

In the meantime, Julian's secretary reported that the photoshoot incident was handled, ascribing the problem to Cornelia's uber-fan. Julian was interested to hear that the fan was Arya's patient, who was also at the hotel the other night. Julian smiled in amusement, saying that Arya's treatment methods were quite unusual.

At the poolside, Cornelia was in an even worse mood than her regular arrogant mode, and her manager nervously called for a break and cleared everyone out. Cornelia made a call to someone perched on a rooftop railing, looking out at the cityscape; this immortal was the guard of air, Caleb, and he quipped that he was there to fly.

Cornelia said, "This is not the time to joke. It's serious. The prince is here. Arkon is here!"

Caleb replied, "Really? The time has come. I didn't expect it would be that fast."

"He said something about the map. I think his servant lost it, so he can't find us. I told you we would be in a big problem. Don't forget you and I are accomplices." Then the call ended. Then she saw Arya's business card and growled jealously that he brought a human woman with him and that the first thing he did in this world was seduce a woman. Caleb, on the other hand, laughed to himself as things were about to get interesting. He stood upon the railing, then jumped off, flying into the air.

Arya took Arkon and Tynar to an office building where they could meet a woman who met immortals frequently. Tynar pulled Arkon aside to ask if it could really lead to Caleb since he had always loved women and debauchery. In any case, Arya led Arkon inside to Nani's office, which has quite the curious setup: the floor was entirely empty but for a tiny box of a shop, whose sign indicated fortune telling. Interesting, considering Nani was Arya's med school friend.

Nani eyed Arkon up and down, then pulled Arya aside to assess the situation. She put together that this was the man who Arya was talking about and that she was the girl who heard voices out of guilt.

Arya explained that he was insistent on meeting an immortal, but he refused a medical approach, so she wanted Nani, who was the closest thing to a person talking to immortals, to figure out what kind of world he lived in so that Arya could help. And yet, Nani said with some amazement that he was the real deal and that he was someone who would be possessed by a real spirit.

Nani sat down with Arkon, who only wanted to know where to find Caleb. She replied that she doesn't know who that is and that she served other immortals. She scattered salt on a tray and named him 'Sigmund Freud'.

Nani rang a bell, listened intently, then lightly touched Arkon's face. She declared that she'd hear him out, but his patience was wearing thin, and he muttered about his foolish servant. He told Nani that he was the next king of Meridian, giving her his royal spiel. As she waited outside, Arya recalled Arkon saying that they were from different worlds and told herself that this was as far as she would go. *Don't get any more involved.* Then her mind flashed to their kiss, and she slapped her head to rid of the thought.

Nani called Arya on her way out of the meeting, telling her to call their old professor, acknowledging that Arkon was a complicated case beyond Arya's abilities.

When Arya returned to Arkon, he asked if she was toying with him with this meeting and said, "I will let you go for good now."

Arya replied, "All I did was not believe a thing that couldn't be believed. This was the best I could do for you."

"How do you differentiate between truth and non-truth?" Arkon asked.

"Your truth is to believe what you want to believe. Your way is easier and less difficult. Some truths cover the eyes that way."

Arya heard her mother's words ringing in her ears: "Your father abandoned us. Think of it that way."

She looked at Arkon with hurt, muttering, "What do you know?" She headed to the stairwell, rattled by Arkon's words and wondering what was so important about the truth.

Suddenly, a dark figure burst out of the door, grabbed Arya, and dragged her into the elevator. Outside the building, Tynar looked up, wondering if he should text Arkon, and saw a struggle unfolding at the edge of the roof. It was the man in black, and he was trying to shove Arya over the ledge as she struggled.

Arkon, meanwhile, was still outside Nani's office when he got a frantic call from Tynar, who narrated what was unfolding on the rooftop: "He's pushing her! She's falling!"

Arkon whirled around to face the windows just as Arya fell down, upside-down, her eyes meeting his.

Arkon raced for the windows, not stopping as he hit the glass, and suddenly, the glass gave way like water as he flew through it easily. Arkon speeded down amidst a stream of water, and Arya outstretched a hand toward him.

Arkon sped his descent until he reached Arya, encircling her in a cocoon of water, and when they reached ground level, the ball of water splashed away into nothing, leaving Arkon standing with Arya cradled in his arms.

Arya stared up at him in utter shock, and the queen's voice said, "It's fate. The one who saves her life once…"

Arya stammered, "W-w-what…?"

Arkon replied, "I told you I am an immortal prince." Arya passed out, and Arkon thought that his powers had come back permanently.

After she passed out, Arkon and Tynar took her to the park because they didn't know where her house was. Tynar was really excited because Arkon's powers had returned because they had suffered in the past few days. Tynar grabbed a small stone and gave it to Arkon; he looked at it, then tried to transform it into a goldstone, but he failed. He realized that his power had vanished again. They couldn't know what the reason behind this was, but it seemed that there was no solution to this problem. In the meantime, Arya fidgeted in her sleep, reliving the encounter from the rooftop in her dreams—how the masked man had dragged her toward the ledge, accusing, "It's all your fault! Because of you, do you know how I lived? Die!"

Arya woke up screaming. She saw Arkon hovering over her and decided she was still in a dream. She closed then opened her eyes again, deciding each time that it was still a dream. When she woke up, she started running out of the park in disbelief. She recalled the sight of Arkon catching her in a swirl of water, but she told herself that it was just her guilty conscience acting up again. But then she remembered her attacker's accusations and froze in her tracks, looking around fearfully as though expecting him to show up at any second. Fending off a panic attack, she ran to her car and crouched there to gather her breath.

A figure in black came up behind her and grabbed her, and Arya tensed and screamed, struggling until she heard Arkon's voice. He had her car keys, and he handed them over, watching as she fumbled with the lock with shaking hands. But she was so rattled that she drove in reverse by accident, then shifted gears and tried to drive while in the park.

Arkon ended up driving, and he advised her to think carefully about who might have attacked her and who may have a grudge against her. Tynar added that it was too bad she couldn't report the incident, given that she couldn't exactly explain how she was saved by a magical prince from another world.

They arrived at Arya's house. Arkon and Tynar walked Arya to her gate. Tynar was shaking with the urge to ask her to let them stay. Because they lived in the park for days, Arya asked if he were truly a magical creature and an immortal. "You're so different from the books I know…"

Arkon turned to go, at which point, Tynar couldn't hold back anymore and shoved him inside the gate and blocked the entrance. He declared that Arya had brought the prince into her home and must allow him to stay. Tynar blocked Arkon from leaving and pressed Arya to answer whether she believed Arkon was an immortal.

Flustered, she said she does, and Tynar warned her that turning away an immortal and the next king of the great world of Meridian would anger him and bring misfortune to her family for generations. Judging from Arkon's smile, it seemed Tynar' was laying it on a little thick.

Then Arya led them to her small rooftop. It was a magnificent view from this roof of the stars, the trees, and the gentle breeze. It was just a perfect spot, but Arkon, who was living in a magical palace, didn't like the place, but he was forced to accept it because it was better than the park. He looked up at the sky, shaking his head…and then glanced down to see a man in black skulking in the alley.

Arya entered her house, and she was freaking out about what happened earlier today. She held her phone and started to search about the legends and the other world theories; she couldn't believe that she was doing that, but she couldn't forget how she fell over a high building and was still alive. Then she called her friend Nani immediately for more advice, only to have Nani unavailable because she was on yet another hobby outing.

In the morning, Arya was struck with a thought, recalling Arkon telling her he could make anything with a flick of his fingers. She headed up to the rooftop but stopped short when she also remembered that he had said that certain circumstances prevented him from doing that now.

She wondered aloud what the circumstances could be, and Tynar chimed in from above to explain. Arya cut him off, saying that she hated hearing about other people's circumstances, just as Tynar's stomach growled loudly.

She took him down to her kitchen and made him breakfast, so he talked to her about Arkon's problem. Arya asked, "Did he come to find a jewel?"

Tynar answered, "Yes, the Great Jewel of Meridian; it's the source of the power of all worlds, and it belongs to the king of Meridian, so he should find the guardians who protect the jewel and take it, and Cornelia is one of those who protects the jewel, so when he finds the jewel, he must go back to be the new king of the immortals' world. Also, it could be a hard mission, but not that much. I don't know why things got very complicated. He also didn't experience something like that in more than 4000 years! And he didn't use hot water for many days. He must be upset now because he used to spend his time in hot lakes."

Arya couldn't believe it and asked, "Has he lived more than 4000 years?" Tynar nodded.

When Tynar went to his part-time job, Arya went to the rooftop a bit later; she freaked out to see Arkon bathing in the large tub. She insisted he get out, but when he started to rise, she screamed and ordered him to stay put, handing him a towel to cover up. Indicating the houses around them, she warned that people would call the police on him if they saw him like this.

He got annoyed at her nagging and reminded her that he was an immortal. Pointing out his powers, she wondered, *Are immortals who lose their powers still immortals?*

Arkon admitted that his powers were touch and go. "But I'm still an immortal anyway." Turning around the question on her, he asked, "If you lose your sense of humanity, would that make you not a human?"

He pointed to the flowers nearby, telling her that he'd jog her memory so that she could know why they kept chattering at her. Then he grabbed Arya around the waist. He yanked her close and loomed over her, warning in a low voice, "Don't you dare test me." Then he let her go. He said that the voices had stopped because she helped him and that they'd start again if she stopped. He said that he wouldn't need much time or expect much help from her in solving his problem—all she has to do is take care of him while he's here. And if she still couldn't accept her duty, he told her to repay him for saving her life.

Arya accepted that deal, preferring to think of herself as returning a favor than being a servant. She issued a few instructions of her own for getting around in the human world, stating that people weren't possessions, and she told him to cut all the 'master' and 'owner' talk. And if he kissed her again, she would report him.

After she left, Arkon noticed that lurker on the street again.

In the meantime, Cornelia worked another fashion shoot, and afterward, she seethed to recall her encounter with Arya and wondered who she was.

Julian, who was the CEO of the resort where Cornelia lived, searched for Cornelia, found her and apologized for the trouble the other day, saying that the doctor went too far trying to help her patient. Cornelia was surprised to hear that he knew Arya, though she wasn't inclined to change her mind about Arya.

Julian made a lousy attempt at a joke, which got no reaction out of Cornelia, and then he made another to his secretary while receiving updates on his projects. He explained being a fan of a particular TV gag program, though he admitted that he doesn't actually find it funny or know why people laugh.

"What I envy about humans the most is their sense of humor. No matter how much I study it, I don't understand it." Then he looked at the papers that his assistant brought to him; he found that Arya's name was listed as a landowner in the area he was developing, finding it curious how he keeps crossing paths with her.

In the meantime, Arya debated whether to report her mysterious attacker, hesitating because of Tynar's remark about not being able to tell the police that an immortal saved her. Arya confided in Nurse Matt about her near-death experience and described how she felt.

"As I fell, I thought I was going to die. But suddenly, the new king of the immortals' world appeared and saved me! He wasn't good-looking."

Matt was shocked about what he just heard, and he put her coffee cup on the desk and asked, "You are not good, Arya. I'm starting to worry about you."

Arya replied, "Who may have a desire to kill me? Are there many people who hate me?"

"Well, there are many people that I can't even count them on my fingers!"

"What? Who?"

"Don't you remember? Our friends, our childhood friends?"

FLASHBACK – ARYA'S CHILDHOOD

Young Arya had interrupted Matt's birthday party to take forkfuls of the cake while they were still singing to him and had declared 'The beggars' cake' to taste bad. On another occasion at school, she'd yanked the jacket off Matt's back, saying it was hers. And another time, Arya had stuffed an entire plate of sausages into her mouth while the orphan kids were eating dinner, leaving none for them.

All these memories hurt Arya because she didn't feel the proper amount of attention from her father because he made his home for orphan kids, so his own daughter felt lost.

In the meantime, Arya left the house key for Arkon and Tynar and gave them access to her fridge, even though that turned out to be only packaged rice and cups of noodles. Arkon dressed less snazzily today. Since a green tracksuit was the only thing available in the recycler, he grudgingly wore it. Arkon said, "Tynar, come, we must go to Arya's clinic. I want her to buy me new clothes because I will not go and see Cornelia in these clothes."

When they arrived at the main street in front of Arya's clinic, they found Arya in the front clinic. Arkon demanded new clothes, saying that Cornelia would find his tracksuit insulting. Matt arrived just then and protested his treatment toward her, which turned into a four-way tug-of-war before Arya yanked free and put a stop to it.

She and Arkon ended up at a department store looking for new clothes, and Arkon vetoed outfit after outfit. She ended up picking a plain suit at a simple neighborhood shop, and Arkon stood huffily outside, miffed that they were not shopping designers.

The shop owner said he should know the adage about the luxury coming from the wearer and that he's got such a great body that he doesn't need to smother it in money. That was one way to appeal his pride.

After buying the suit, Arya suggested grabbing a bite to eat, and Arkon said loftily that immortals don't feel trifling feelings like hunger.

"But I saw you in the park making a fight for a chicken wing," she said though and even made a mocking hungry face at him. Then Arkon's stomach betrayed a growl, contradicting his words.

He refused to eat the noodles she bought him, even his stomach continued to rumble, so Arya literally shoved the food into his mouth. He protested but did end up picking up his utensils to eat, however grudgingly.

Arya asked if Cornelia would really help this time, and he replied, "Yes," without hesitation, having full confidence that she would come through. Arya seemed the teeniest bothered by his faith in Cornelia, but Arkon asked why she didn't have someone like that in her life—someone to trust and depend on no matter what. She replied that he'd understand how pointless it is once you've been betrayed by someone you trusted.

Arkon noticed how Arya warmed up her cold water with hot, and she explained that she disliked cold water. He asked if it was winter when she threw herself into the water and why she tried to die. Startled, she denied it, but he was pretty insightful and guessed it was because of the one who betrayed her.

As they left the restaurant, Arkon spotted a businessman lingering outside, who hastily turned away upon being spotted. Arkon commented that it was problematic for his servant to be afraid of the water. Arya balked again at being called a servant. She proposed a deal where they exchange favors, with hers being that he stop calling her servant. Arkon didn't have a favor to ask but did offer a warning.

"Don't fall in love with me," he said, leaning close. "If you fall in love with me, there's no cure." Arya stared at him with exasperation, thinking that there was no cure for 'him'!

In the meantime, Matt called her, "Where are you? Come to the clinic right now."

"What happened?"

"There is a buyer for your piece of land!" Arya rushed to the clinic. When she arrived, she found Matt waiting for her in front of the clinic. She first asked about the buyer. Matt answered, "You will not believe that Mr. Julian's company called me and told me that they want to buy your land because it's important for their new project."

She didn't believe that luck was smiling at her again. She said, "Oh, shall I ask for more money? Shall I request five times its price?" In the meantime, the phone rang. She got a call from Julian's secretary. She caught herself before seeming too eager and forced an airy tone, telling the secretary to have Julian call her directly. She figured this was her chance to play the upper hand, and although she betrayed the tiniest bit of anxiousness while waiting for the phone to ring, luckily for her, it did.

At that time in the luxurious resort, Arkon and Tynar headed over to find Cornelia, who spotted them first across from a distance and looked displeased about it. Tynar complained that Arkon was too easy on Cornelia, which was why she got away with her behavior, and added that if she were to learn he'd lost his powers, she'd look down on him even more. They didn't know that she heard everything they said. Arkon informed Tynar to keep that part a secret from her, but she got out from behind and surprised them.

Cornelia said, "You lost what?"

Arkon turned to her and replied, "It's a matter of time; it will come back. I want to know why you did that the last time you saw me. Why didn't you recognize me?"

She replied, "Let's go to my apartment; let's talk there." When they first arrived, Tynar started to cry, complaining about everything that had happened to them.

"It was very hard for us. The prince lost his powers once he arrived in this world, and we couldn't find a way to see you or the other guards because we lost the map, and we had no place to stay. The only one good thing was that we met Arya, who gave us a place to stay and bought us these cell phones—"

Arkon interrupted him and said, "I want to live here. Where are Caleb and Van? I want the jewel. Give it to me right now."

She stared at him and said, "No! I will not give you the jewel, and I don't know where Caleb and Van are. Also, I will not allow you to live here!"

Arkon shouted, "How dare you talk with me like that? I'm your king!"

She stood and said, "Do you forget the guards' mission to protect the Jewel of Meridian, and it's up to us if we want to give you the jewel or not."

Tynar countered, "Please, my lady, calm down. That is not allowed. The guard's mission is to protect the jewel and give it to the next king. You can't do this."

She yelled, "How dare you interfere, you idiot servant! How dare you talk like that? Also, there are a lot of things that have changed here. Living in a world of humans in this crazy era changed a lot of things; we are not in Meridian."

Arkon was controlling his nerves very hard. Then Cornelia said, "In the last few years and before the jewel was sent, we created a new method to protect it when it came, so I, Caleb, and Van created three magical stones to protect the jewel and hide it when it came here because we were busy protecting the veil between the worlds."

Arkon asked, "Okay, then give me the three stones. It will lead me to the location of the jewel."

Her facial expressions changed as she was scared, then she said, "How should I trust you? You lost your powers. If you were qualified to be a king, you would see Caleb and Van standing in front of you." Arkon felt great anger; he stood to leave, then he walked back to her. Arkon asked what he would have to do to earn Cornelia's approval and get the stone, pressing her with increasing insistence until she blurted, "Report all the hateful comments about me on the internet!" Arkon didn't know what that was, but she tried to find something to make him busy. Clearly, she hid something.

He got out with Tynar and saw Arya, who had come to meet Julian to sell her land to him. When Arya saw him, she was surprised, but she remembered that he told her he would come back to the resort to see Cornelia.

Meanwhile, Cornelia whined to Caleb over the phone about her encounter, embarrassed at her own request, blaming it on her surprise. Caleb guessed she was flustered to have Arkon ask to do something for her, which she hotly denied.

Arkon approached Arya and asked her, "What is a bodyguard?" It turned out that Cornelia had also demanded that he be her bodyguard at her fan signing. Arya noticed that Cornelia was acting a lot more like a prissy middle-schooler than an immortal. In the meantime, Julian came and saw Arya with Arkon.

He approached and said, "I see that you are not alone. I hope we will negotiate and make the best deal." Arya couldn't speak in front of Arkon. She felt uncomfortable. When Julian saw her like that, he said, "If the time is not suitable for you, we can arrange another meeting for you."

Arya replied immediately, "No, no, it's good." Then she turned to Arkon, said see you later, and walked with Julian.

Arkon didn't feel well. He felt something was wrong with Julian, but he didn't utter a single word. Tynar said, "It looks like her friend has a lot of gold." While Arya and Julian were walking, he received a phone call. His assistant told him that he could meet Mr. Hale now.

Julian ended the call and gave Arya an envelope containing the contract and said, "This is the contract; please read it. It gives you seven times the land value. I will go now."

Arya came back to the clinic, and she was delighted; she couldn't believe that her problems were going to end because of the rocky land. She told Matt, "I will be busy because I will sell everything and travel to the island that I have dreamt of." She caught her necklace and said, "Do you know I found this necklace beside my bed on one of those nights when I slept while I was crying? That's why I loved it very much. I felt it was a gift from God to me." She stared at Matt and said, "Don't worry; I will find you a good job after leaving the clinic. Now I want you to come with me; we will celebrate."

In the meantime, Arkon and Tynar were at the rooftop, talking about the hateful comments. Tynar was reading the comments on Cornelia's posts on the internet. He told Arkon how to report these comments. They didn't know that Cornelia was stalling them. Arkon asked, "Why hasn't Arya come back yet?"

Tynar replied, "She will come soon." Then they heard men's voices.

Arkon asked, "What is that?"

"These are men voices; they get drunk and make fights between them, my lord. There are a lot of strange things happening at night in the human world," Tynar replied. Arkon was thinking about the man who had been following them for the past few days. He felt worried about Arya.

In the meantime, Arya finished celebrating with Matt. She came back, walking alone on the streets, staring at the people: the kids with their parents, the couples, the old people. She suffered from being alone for most of her life. She crossed beside a chicken shop and remembered Arkon and rushed to buy him a chicken meal. She came back to her home. She was carrying the chicken box when she arrived at her home. She was surprised to see Arkon waiting for her under the yellow streetlight; she approached him slowly. When she saw his face, she smiled immediately. Whenever she concentrated on him, she couldn't believe the amount of beauty. Then she asked, "What are you doing here?" He gave the excuse that he was just thinking of how to get his powers back, but as they walked together, she pointed back up the street and told him to try waiting there next time.

Arkon turned his nose up at her offer of chicken, insisting that he didn't need food…just as his stomach grumbled. Arya tested out a theory, saying the word 'food' over and over and hearing his stomach growl in response each time.

She urged him to accept that he was an immortal who could sense hunger, and then she pranked him by jumping at him from around the corner. He wondered about her good mood, and she explained, "I met a real king. A real king who will save me from this earth's hell."

Arkon's mind flashed to Julian, then he asked, "Who is being deceived now? Being good-looking doesn't make everyone a king."

Arya replied, "A king is a superior being who makes people's desperate wishes come true. That is the real king."

Arkon said he was the real deal, and she just agreed dismissively and asked how his comment-hunt was going, then recalled that he couldn't read. Arkon picked up a rock from the ground and used it to scratch out her name on the brick wall, followed by his own name. He missed a letter and spelled 'Arkon', so Arya added in the missing piece. Upon the rooftop, the three, Arya, Arkon, and Tynar, sat to eat the grilled chicken. Arkon tried to resist again, but Arya put the chicken leg in his hand, then he immediately bit it.

Arya stared at Arkon and said, "I don't know how things go on in your world, and I also don't know the rules and how they live there, but I know that in the past few weeks you experienced hunger, betrayal, and deprivation. I think all these things are destined to happen to make you the best king."

Arkon spoke no word because he didn't feel gratitude for what happened, but now, after hearing that, he saw it differently.

She asked, "Do you know what a bodyguard means?"

"Yes, I learned what that means; there is a movie called The Good Bodyguard, and I feel it's fun. Also, it's worth it to experience that," Arkon replied.

Arya looked at him and thought, *You are going to regret that.*

The next day, Arkon and Tynar got attacked by a horde of fans clamoring to get closer to Cornelia. They yanked his hair and shoved him to the ground. He didn't expect that at all. Inside the van, Arkon asked, "Are you going to continue doing this to me?"

"I'm sorry, I can't. I can't trust in the heir who lost his power!" Arkon felt great anger and left with Tynar.

Cornelia called Caleb. "I can't do that anymore; do it yourself." Then she ended the call.

In a bad mood because of his day, Arkon demanded the car from Arya, wanting to relieve stress with a drive. She refused, but when he threatened to find another car on the internet, she only knew how that would end up—she ended up bringing the car out reluctantly. She didn't let him drive, though, and asked pointedly if there were any instructions online on how to kill an immortal. She agreed to go on the drive since she could use the relief too but firmly ignored Arkon's insistence on taking the wheel, so off she drove, heading toward the beach for a walk out in the fresh air. They walked on the beach and captured many photos. Then they went to a grassy field, where Tynar ran around like a child, and Arkon lay down for a rest.

Arya stretched out and lay down next to Arkon, sighing that she had a rough day and that it would be nice if he had his powers. She asked if he'd be able to make coral, sand, and sunlight. She said sleepily, "I'd like to go into the ocean. I see…the ocean."

In Arya's mind, she saw herself swimming in the sea and said that she was not scared of the water, nor was she lonely, even though she was alone. Suddenly, Arkon appeared next to her in the water, saying that it was no good for her to be alone. She replied, "I wanted to be alone."

In her dream, they swam together underwater, and he placed his hand on her back to guide her along. She asked what he was doing, and he replied that she doesn't know how to swim.

Back in the real world, Arkon watched her, propped up on one arm. He said, "I'm sorry."

Arya opened her eyes, turned to look at him, and asked, "For what?"

He didn't answer her, then said, "Let's go."

Chapter Five
They Lost It

When they walked to the car to leave, a car passed, and Arkon recognized the driver as the same man who seemed to be following Arya the other day. Arkon watched as the suspicious man tampered with Arya's car's engine and tires. Having studied up on cars, Arkon deduced that the man was trying to cause an accident by making Arya's brakes fail.

Arkon didn't say anything, so when they rode the car, Arkon asked for the keys and plunked himself down in the driver's seat. Arya argued at first, then relented and climbed in the back seat, and they drove off as the suspicious man watched them go. Arkon drove like a madman, purposely pushing the car and ignoring Arya's panicked screeching. He whipped across the lanes and then ran a red light, missing another car by inches, while Arya lectured him that not everyone in the car is immortal.

Finally, Arkon agreed to slow down, but when he hit the brakes, nothing happened. Arya started to panic for real as the car picked up speed, and Arkon struggled to keep control.

Things looked terrible as they approached a tunnel that was blocked off for construction, but Arkon thought, *Wait, woman. Do you think that I'll let my servant die so easily?* As Arya begged him to do something, Arkon tried using his powers and ordered the car to stop, but it didn't work.

They went barreling through the pylons and into the tunnel. Seeing the other end blocked by trucks, Arkon analyzed the situation and devised another plan. He opened the sunroof and told Tynar to hold onto the wheel. Then he climbed up to the roof of the moving car. Then he reached a hand down to Arya, and she looked up at his face, and he gave her a tiny nod. She clasped Arkon's hand, and he pulled her to the roof beside him. She asked, "What are you planning to do?"

He replied calmly, "We're going to jump."

After telling Tynar to get himself out, Arkon stood and hoisted Arya into his arms. He leaned close to her and whispered, "Don't be scared. You are under my protection." Then Arkon jumped straight up, and a giant bubble of air materialized around him and Arya, lifting them into the air. After a long moment, Arya opened her eyes and saw a magical thing surrounding them. Then the bubble gently lowered them to the pavement. Arkon asked, "Are you okay?"

But then the car slammed into the trucks at the end of the tunnel and exploded. But…Tynar was in there! Arkon looked a little shocked, and he told Arya over and over that it was okay.

He finally set Arya down, and a few seconds later, a charred but okay Tynar ran up. Oh, Tynar wailed that Arkon's powers had returned. Then he grabbed a rock for Arkon to test himself. Arkon dropped the stone, already aware that his powers had left him again. He thought, *Why are my powers back when only Arya needs me?*

He stared at Arya and said, "We must file a report to the police!"

Arya interrupted and asked, "A report?"

"Yes, there is someone who tampered with your car's brakes. Also, I saw that in a movie! You said that the CCTV cameras are everywhere, so the police can check them out."

The police caught him very fast by seeing the cameras when Arya went to the police station and saw the man. She recognized him as the same man she recently bumped into on the street, who'd acted offended at her frightened reaction. The cop said, "He admitted that he wanted to kill you. You parked the car in a place that appeared in the cameras, and everything has been captured. Do you know him?"

She stated, "Actually, yes, and no. I only met him three days ago on the street—"

The cop revealed, "You had a car accident three months ago; do you remember that? He was the other driver."

Arya was shocked and said, "Yes, that was the same day that I found the necklace!"

The cop said, "Sorry, what?"

She replied, "No, nothing." Then she added, "After the incident, I didn't see the man ever again because the insurance companies handled everything."

Arkon was silent throughout this conversation, watching the man shrewdly through the one-way glass. The cop said the guy was nuts because he insisted that the car accident was a permanent blemish on his life, which he'd lived perfectly until that moment. Another cop got inside the room and said, "This man is crazy. He said that he pushed her from a high building a few days ago, but she didn't die." Arya looked at him and remembered that accident, and she was shocked. Then the cop continued.

"The man said that she is not a human; that's why he insisted on killing her!"

After they left the police office, Arkon said, "You should relax now and be calm because they found the criminal who tried to kill you; you can focus now only on serving me!"

She looked at him and said, "Sorry, but I'm not feeling good. I must go somewhere." She left him and walked alone, thinking about what was happening to her. She couldn't imagine that she could die today or in a few days. She felt that she needed to go to a calm place, looking for answers. She went to a small street with old houses. The trees were tall around the old-fashioned houses everywhere. She remained walking until she arrived at a large wooden door; she pushed the door and entered. There was a huge building covered by green plants; no one seeing the street would expect a huge place like that.

She opened the internal door, and there was a massive hall behind it, and the books were everywhere, from the ground to the roof. She walked to see what she came for. The place was empty; no voices were heard; no people were seen. She felt scared. Then a hand touched her left shoulder. She froze and turned slowly. A tall man with long golden hair, green eyes, and round glasses spoke calmly.

"I'm Cedric. I'm the librarian of this place. How can I help you?"

Arya thought he was a magical creature; she couldn't speak at first, then she shook her head and said, "Thank you. I'm looking for legendary books on immortals and these sorts of things. Can you please tell me where I can find them?"

He raised his hand and pointed at the corner shelf. Arya looked at his strange ring with a tree sign on it, then she said, "Thank you." She walked toward the shelf and searched every single book. Then the man came to her and gave her a book and said, "You are looking for that book." She took it, and she was surprised at how he could know the book. She looked at the book's title and froze in her place when she read 'The World of Meridian'. She immediately looked at the librarian, but she couldn't see him; he had vanished like he wasn't there!

She took the book and got out of the place; she read it while she was going back home. Everything was written down in this book with all the details; it was like the writer was living there. She wondered how could such a book be on earth! *Who wrote this book? Who brought it here?* Arya wondered.

She came back to her home and found Arkon and Tynar on the rooftop. She said, "I told you not to take a shower here. That's not allowed."

Arkon replied, "I saved your life twice!" Tynar told Arya that back in Meridian, Arkon was known to sit in the hot lake for an entire day. Ignoring their complaints, Arkon commanded Arya to provide him with a bubble bath, a new phone as it was destroyed in the car crash, new clothes, and better food.

When Arya left for the market to buy all the things that Arkon wanted, Tynar said, "What if you were wrong? What if your power didn't come back then? You would put Arya's life in grave danger!"

"I wondered about that, and I wanted to be sure about it, and I know now that my powers come back only when she needs my help," Arkon replied.

Arya came back, and she tried to cook different types of food, but she couldn't; all the meals that she made had failed; some of them burned, the other had no taste. Arkon saw her, and he was watching a cooking TV show, so he went to the kitchen, then expertly tied on an apron and got to work, handling the food like he had spent years studying the culinary arts.

Then they all sat down to eat the delicious-looking meal. Arkon refused to look at Arya as he cut his steak; then he switched plates with her. His unexpected chivalry took Arya back, and she said he didn't need to do things like that. Then Arkon added a slice of apple to her plate, calling it a token of his apology.

After dinner, Arkon and Arya enjoyed a glass of wine. Arya was thinking of her attacker again, whom she guessed had a form of obsessive-compulsive disorder, driving him to seek perfection. She admitted to feeling guilty for ignoring his attempts to reach her, which were probably a cry for help. Noting that the same thing had happened with the patient who jumped into the river, Arya said that she didn't want to feel responsible or sorry for things like these. She admitted that she only wanted to think of herself.

Arkon said, "You will not have this life!"

"Why?" Arya asked.

"Because that's not the sort of person you are." He continued, "When you ride a bicycle, in order not to fall, you have to turn the handle in the direction it's falling in." He asked Arya, "Isn't it just that you're unaware of which direction your heart is trying to fall? If you keep trying to force yourself to steer in the other direction, you'll fall over and grow ill."

Arya thought, *This is the first time that this 4000-year-old immortal has said something wise!* She remained silent, and Arkon stared at her red hair and her white cotton face. He didn't notice before how beautiful this girl was.

Arkon walked toward Tynar, who was about to fall off the wooden bed, but Arya reached out and grabbed his shirt again. This time, Arkon didn't slap her hand away, and they shared a charged moment as he looked into her eyes. Arya said, "Thank you for saving me again…and for keeping me busy today."

In the meantime, in Julian's office, he was studying books on humor late into the night. He took a break to smile over his many, so many trophies and awards, and he told himself that once he nails this humor thing, he'll be perfect.

His assistant, Secretary Nigel, called him to fuss at him for staying up late studying again, calling this obsession with human behavior a symptom of having no family. He suggested Julian to date instead, but Julian told him to get to the point. Secretary Nigel mentioned a few schedule changes for tomorrow.

In a private swimming pool, a man with vigorous steps, brown hair, and gray eyes walked inside and saw Cornelia in the pool. When she first saw him, she said, "Caleb! I told you not to come here, but you never listen."

"Can't you be nicer to me? It's been a long time since I saw you last time."

He noticed her cranky mood and wondered if she had to go back to the realm of the immortals. "Do you want to see that jerk, the one the high priest told us about when we were little, the immortal who said he'd kill everyone?"

Caleb's usual impish grin faded to a snarl as Cornelia asked if he still believed the stories he was told as a child. Then she asked, "Do you have a plan for what we should tell the prince? I don't think that we can lie for too long." He thought, then suggested they both tell Arkon that they'd give him their magical stone if the other gave their first.

"I can't believe that I'm agreeing to be in your silly plan. I don't know what he would do when he discovered that we were lying to him. I think this plan will not work out."

"Even so, that will buy us a little time. Where is he now?" Caleb asked.

Cornelia grumbled that he was using a human servant for the first time in the history of immortals, tossing Arya's business card to him. Caleb read Arya's name and smiled to see that the servant was a woman, then he said, "I know someone carrying the same name!"

The next morning, Arya woke up, and it took her several minutes to realize that she was in Arkon's rooftop room. She freaked out when she saw Arkon sitting on the couch a few feet away. Then he told her that she got drunk on dessert wine last night and crawled her way into his room. So Arya rushed out, and the corner of Arkon's mouth quirked up in a satisfied smile. When Arkon followed her out, Tynar made the natural assumption, but Arya just stammered out of denial and ran downstairs. In the meantime, Tynar's phone rang. When he picked up, he heard Caleb's voice. He immediately said, "Lord Caleb!"

Caleb replied, "I heard that Prince Arkon is with you. Tell him that I want to see him. Let him come to my place."

When the call ended, Tynar told Arkon what Caleb had told him, but he added, "I think it's better you go there, and you have your power back, but we can't put Arya's life in danger again. I felt pity that we tricked her last time." A voice came from the roof's door, and it was Arya.

She said, "What? What does that mean?" She walked toward Arkon, stepped in front of him, and barked, "Are you trying to kill me? That's why you apologized before, right? All that to regain your stupid powers again?"

He looked at her and replied, "My stupid powers!"

She answered, "Yes, I don't know how great your powers are, and I don't want to know, but you can't risk a valuable human life to regain it or to be sure of a stupid theory." She left, and Tynar followed her.

He said, "He knew that his power would come back and save you—"

"What if not? What would happen to me?"

"He would save you, no matter how much it would cost him. Don't forget that he saved your life twice."

In the meantime, Arkon came down from the stairs and yelled, "Tynar, let's go!" They went to the main street, where the taxi was waiting for them. Arya followed them and got in the car with them. Arkon looked at her.

She said, "What? I'm coming with you. I want your friend to pay me back. I spent a lot of money, and I saved all the bills!"

When they arrived at Caleb's building, where he lived in the penthouse, Arya marveled that these immortals live such high-profile lives in the human world. Shooting Arkon the side-eye, she wondered if the world was in such a shameful state because the immortals were living like this, and he snapped that she was getting ruder. Arya said, "This building reminds me of someone I know—the man who gave me a diamond ring that I lost on the day I first met you. He was such a good man; he loved me very much. Unfortunately, he left the college before graduating." Arkon didn't like what he heard and walked to the building's gate.

They ended up at the penthouse. When Caleb opened the door, he immediately smiled at Arya's face. Then Arkon said, "It's been a long time, Caleb."

Caleb said, "I can't believe it's you, Arya!" Arya realized that her friend who gave her the diamond ring years ago was the same immortal whom Arkon was looking for. Then she fainted immediately.

Caleb smiled fondly at Arya as she slept. He expressed disbelief that his old friend was the immortal's servant, guessing that that was why he was so attracted to her. His sweet smile disappeared as he turned to Arkon. With a snap of his fingers, Caleb made Arkon's wine fly out of his glass and splash into Tynar's face. He said cheekily that divine nature doesn't disappear because you lose your powers. He was curious since he never lost his.

Arkon stated, "Cornelia said that you created magical stones to protect the jewel when it comes to this world. Give me your stone."

"I will not give you anything. If you want, you can take Cornelia's stone first, and then I will think about giving you mine." Arya roused from her sleep, and the first thing she saw was Caleb looking at her with a happy grin. Her eyes went wide, and she passed out again.

Arkon admitted that after having felt betrayal, he also felt hunger. Borrowing Arya's words, he said that he felt like a better king now than he was yesterday and the day before that. "I'm learning to be a great king. That's why I lost my powers."

Arkon and Tynar stood to leave, but Caleb told them to let Arya sleep there so they could catch up. He reached down to her, but Arkon grabbed his wrist, and they stared angrily into each other's eyes. Arkon piggybacked Arya into the elevator, looking supremely annoyed.

In the meantime, Secretary Nigel was helping Julian plant a tree, and they discussed Arya's reluctance to sign the sale papers for her land. Julian understood that she'd have a hard time selling something that's belonged to her family for so long. He said that Arya is really a very good-hearted person, but she doesn't want anyone to know. Secretary Nigel replied that wasn't his question, but Julian cut him off to say that it was fun watching her pretend to be evil. He asked if that answered Secretary Nigel's question, revealing that the secret to his success was that he was analyzing people's feelings.

Finally, Arya woke up in her own bed, thinking that she was waking for the first time since getting drunk on the roof and assuming that the fight with Arkon and seeing Caleb again were all a dream. She wandered downstairs to find Arkon on her couch, eyes closed. She was about to smack him when he said, "I heard that diamond ring wasn't a proposal ring." He smirked, saying that it was a friendship ring and that Caleb gave twenty of them to different people. Arya started to faint again, but Arkon yelled, "DON'T FAINT!" He snapped her out of it.

Arkon warned Arya away from Caleb, but she was stuck in a semi-daze. Arkon poked her and told her that Caleb was born on the back of the immortal of love and that he enjoys betrayal. Tynar said they should talk to Cornelia again and wondered where someone named Van was. They tried talking to Cornelia, who had to brace herself before approaching Arkon. He clearly made her nervous as he chided her for telling Caleb about his lost powers, then asked for her stone again. Cornelia stammered that she couldn't, then she flinched away from Arkon's outstretched hand. She told him that she'd give him her stone once he got Caleb's and rushed back to her car, laying her head on the wheel and whining that she was sorry. A voice from the backseat startled her. Then she turned to see Caleb looking pleased with the idea of ganging up on Arkon again. He vaguely mentioned their proposal, which he said was still valid, adding that it was not making Arkon jealous as Cornelia had hoped.

In the meantime, Arya fidgeted in her office, her mind on Caleb. Matt came to fuss at her for not answering Julian's calls, so she made arrangements to meet him and sell her land.

On the drive back to the city, Arkon told Tynar that he had read up on Arya's profession and that he had something to ask her regarding the mental states of Cornelia and Caleb because they had been in the world of humans for too long.

On her way to see Julian, Arya was startled by Caleb, who appeared in front of her suddenly. He said that he wanted to hear more about her being the immortals' servant. Then he took her by the wrist and shoved her into his car, locking the door with a snap of his fingers. As he got into the car, Caleb beheld eyes with Arkon, who had just arrived there. Without a moment's hesitation, Arkon chased Caleb's car on foot, but Caleb pressed on the gas and left Arkon in the dust. From the overpass, Julian, who had come to see Arya, looked down at Arkon with an interesting expression on his face.

Caleb drove so fast that the world outside the car faded into a blur. He screeched to a stop on a bridge, and Arya jumped out to dry-heave. Telling Arya to wait there, Caleb flew up to the top of the bridge, then waved his arms to the gathering storm clouds and said, "No, it's not the time to rain; disappear."

Then he added, "We are the veil guardians. We are great, but you humans destroy everything. If you will continue to ignore the warnings of nature, you will destroy this planet." Arya thought, *What is he talking about? Oh my God, he's crazier than before!*

Caleb mused that all of the humans who received a ring from him lived well except her, and he asked if she threw it out.

Caleb flew back down and said that he needed a favor. Holding out a tiny vial, he said that if she gets Arkon to ingest the red liquid inside, the ring is hers. And her life will change to the best version. He explained that it would make Arkon temporarily forget the magical stones and give himself time to take care of something. He offered Arya one wish in addition to the ring, saying that he could even make her rich.

She took the vial as Caleb warned her to be careful with it since it was the only one in existence. With a huff of disdain, Arya dropped the vial and then crushed it under her shoe. She told Caleb haughtily that her wish wasn't to be rich.

Angry, Caleb informed Arya that she's not Arkon's servant. She's 'every' immortal's servant. He told her that Arkon couldn't do anything for her without his powers, but Arya countered that Arkon's powers aren't entirely gone!

In the meantime, Cornelia drove Arkon and Tynar to find Caleb, annoyed that they were going to this trouble. Then she gasped and asked Arkon if this was 'because of that girl', but Arkon stayed silent.

They found Caleb and Arya on the bridge, and Arkon nervously gestured to Arya to come to him. She tried, but Caleb waved his hand and sent her flying backward. The concrete cracked around her in a circle and crumbled down to the river way down below, trapping her on a floating island of concrete in the middle of the bridge as both Arkon and Cornelia screamed at Caleb.

Caleb offered Arkon a deal—show him his powers, and he'll reconsider giving him the magical stone. When Arkon hesitated, Caleb snapped and caused a thunderstorm to break right over Arya's head. Arkon tried to run to her, but Caleb threatened to send her into the river if he took one more step. Caleb told

Cornelia, "She told me that the prince's powers come back when she is in danger! Aren't you curious about that?"

Cornelia replied, "What? Is that right?"

Arkon shook with fury as Arya screamed in fear and rage. Tynar yelled to Arkon that he was not allowed to harm humans, but Caleb reminded him that the immortals' servants were an exception to that rule.

He raised his fingers for another snap. Caleb told the seething Arkon that it was his turn to act. But then, in a deceptively calm voice, Arkon said, "You lost the magical stones, didn't you?" That knocked Caleb's confidence right out from under him, and the pavement underneath Arya repaired itself in seconds as the storm ended.

Caleb and Cornelia looked genuinely frightened as Arkon asked, "Why did you lose the stones? That means we lost the great Jewel of Meridian…"

Chapter Six
Ancient Memories

Arkon demanded to know what happened to the stones, and as Caleb began to deny it, Cornelia said, "He lost it. It's not my fault."

"Cornelia, why did you give up so fast?" Caleb asked.

She continued, "He lost it and suggested using each other as an excuse."

Tynar asked, "Is that true? Did you lose the stones? That's why you didn't want to give it back to us."

Cornelia said, "He asked me to hide this from you. He said that you would never forgive us if we lost the stones that protect the jewel."

Arya staggered to her feet, brushing away Tynar's attempt to help. She slowly approached Caleb, then nailed him with a strong left hook to his face. Sobbing, she walked up to Arkon, giving him a heartbreaking look of betrayal, then she got into Cornelia's car and drove off with it.

Caleb found the situation hilarious. When Cornelia started to explain, Arkon said darkly that they'd discuss it tomorrow. He followed Caleb to his car and punched him hard enough to knock him to the ground. He admitted that was a true punch. Caleb held up his arms in mocking surrender, but his outstretched hand was ignored by both Arkon and Cornelia. They got in the backseat. Tynar eventually helped Caleb stand, and Caleb muttered that Arkon's fist still feels the same.

At Cornelia's place near the pool, Cornelia paced while Caleb swam, and suddenly, he remembered something that happened two thousand years ago. Arkon had given him and Cornelia each a water firefly to play with, but they'd lost them. They'd tried the same tactic of refusing to give theirs back until the other did first, and when Arkon discovered that they'd lost the fireflies, he'd punched Caleb and nearly turned Cornelia into a beast.

Cornelia said, "Are you stupid to use the same method again!"

"Didn't you know? Yes, I'm stupid." Caleb replied.

"You always made problems, even when we were in Meridian. You made Queen Wera punish Arya's ancestors only to bother Arkon because of his ancient problems with the human girl."

Cornelia wondered why Arkon wanted to talk to them tomorrow instead of immediately, and Caleb crowed that he had more important things to worry about today!

In the meantime, Arya didn't return home by evening, and Arkon stood on the roof obsessing over the danger she was in today and how he couldn't help her. He looked miserable. Meanwhile, Arya visited her mother's grave, and she sat for a while, idly pulling weeds and chatting.

She asked her mother if she knew their family descended from servants of the immortals, wondering if it was her mother's or her father's side of the family. She told her mother that so much was happening lately but that she had nobody to talk to about it. She mentioned Nani and Matt, remembering Matt as the most cowardly and annoying of the orphans her father took in. Arya said that she's still not heard from her father and that she knew he was not missing but was just choosing not to come back, though she admitted that she longed for closure.

When she returned home, Arkon eventually went downstairs to the alley, where Arya found him waiting for her under the streetlight. She started to walk past him, but when he asked if she was okay, she rounded on him angrily and asked what terrible deed her ancestor did to render her life a toy for the immortals.

Arkon's eyes filled with grief. Arya said, "Let me tell you something. It's right that my life is not joyful or even important. I even didn't have the time to think about it—future, dreams—I think I was thinking of these things at some point in my life, but that faded long ago. I'm paying now the cost of a dream I couldn't afford; my life is miserable enough to care for you or the others, but that doesn't mean I don't care how I will die."

Arya's eyes started to pour tears, then she continued, "You said that you are an immortal and from a very faraway world with strong powers, then fulfill my wish! Let me see my father; let me meet him. I want to ask him why he left me all these troubles that weigh on me and if he could sleep at night and eat well since he left. I want to know…why he left; how could he save the world if he couldn't save his daughter?"

Then she walked, but Arkon caught her hand and said, "I promise you I will not let your life be in danger in the cause of what we are doing. I promise you that I will protect you, and this is my duty, a king's duty."

She hesitated and replied, "Actually, I want to be great and say I can protect myself, but honestly, I can't bear all of you, so yes, promise me and make sure to keep your word."

Arkon stated, "I will. I give my word."

She entered her home thinking about Arkon. Arkon went to the rooftop, also thinking about her. Then he remembered what Arya's ancestor did…

FLASHBACK – 1150 YEARS AGO

In a magical spot somewhere in Meridian, Queen Wera sat on the throne, and Arkon stood behind her, and the guards were around them. Also, there was a man with his son. They bowed on the ground in front of the queen, begging her to forgive them. The man said, "My queen, forgive me, and my family will be your servants."

The queen replied, "No, not only your current family."

She decreed that he and all of his descendants would be required to serve the immortals. Not only that but the man's descendants would only have one child and that the descendant's spouse would die after the child was born.

END FLASHBACK

The next morning, Arya found Arkon bathing on the roof again. She averted her eyes as he wrapped himself in a towel, and once he was decently covered, she asked where she could find Cornelia to return her car. Arkon said it was his car now. He ordered Cornelia to transfer the title to Arya since Arkon didn't have a license. But he made it clear that it was his car because he was immortal and not subject to human laws. Arya avoided his grabs for the keys and headed off to work in her snazzy new ride.

In the meantime, Miranda parked at Julian's building. Chairman Hale yelled at her over the phone for causing a scandal and creating rumors that Julian is her boyfriend. He said it was a good thing they were related, but Miranda replied that changing Julian's surname to their family's name doesn't make him from the family. Miranda learned from her manager that she was expected to give an interview today with Julian to dispel the rumors. She was annoyed that she nearly walked in front of a car and the car almost hit her, and the driver turned out to be Secretary Nigel, who calmly said that she was on the road.

He refused to listen to her spoiled whining and informed her that Julian wouldn't be giving statements today.

When Arya arrived at work, Matt leaped at her, upset that she didn't show up for her meeting with Julian yesterday. He's also moped because she didn't call him and let him know what was happening, and he asked how he was supposed to face her father when he returns.

Arya ran to her office to call Julian, but Matt let him in a few seconds later because he came to see her in person. Arya told him about how something came up and her phone broke, but Julian quieted her with a gentle touch on the wrist, just relieved that she was okay. Arya wanted to sign the sale contract, but she suddenly remembered that she accidentally left it in Caleb's car when he came and took her yesterday. Julian declined to hear her explanation, just saying that he understood and that he'd wait for her to contact him.

Arya promised to visit him that evening to sign the papers. But a strange look came over Julian's face, and he said, "I will be in a very private place tonight."

Meanwhile, Arkon went to see Cornelia and Caleb at Caleb's place. They sat down to explain everything that had happened to them. Cornelia said, "Sorry."

Arkon looked at her and replied, "Tell me everything."

"Well, that wasn't my mistake. It's all Caleb's!" Cornelia replied. Then she continued, "We told you that we created the stones when we felt the jewel would be sent here. So we created it nine years ago because we didn't think that the jewel would be delayed, so on that day, we needed a compelling environment, so we went to the place of the gate. Once we were there, Caleb and I fought over a silly thing, and Van (the third guardian) used his power to stop us. So that made a big explosion, and the stones disappeared between the worlds, which means when the time of the new king came and the jewel was sent here, the stones used their powers and hid it in the safest place for the jewel, but we couldn't find the place without the stones. Since that day, the stones have been missing, but Van immediately went to search for them between the worlds, and we haven't seen him since that day!"

Arkon couldn't believe what he heard and asked, "Van's been missing for nine years, and you didn't search for him? And why did you create the stones? Why did you change the order?"

Caleb replied, "You can't blame us. You didn't live here. This world is crazy. We were protecting the veil to prevent humans from finding their way to other worlds because they destroy everything they touch. We were fixing all the natural problems. The water is poisoned because of humans, also the air and everything, so we couldn't handle all of that. That's why we created the magical stones. We didn't know that would happen."

When Arkon and Cornelia left Caleb's penthouse, Cornelia again whined that she really did try to find the missing stones. She told Arkon that everyone knows how Van tends to disappear when he's focused on something. She said that day Van had said something was strange and requested that they come to meet him at the magical gate. Arkon asked what was strange, but Cornelia nervously admitted that she never found out because she and Caleb were fighting.

Cornelia asserted, "Don't worry; we will find the stones, and everything will be all right. Caleb knows a lot of magical servants living here. He will order them to search for the stones." Then she continued, "The problem is not about Tynar losing the map. It's about the original law and why the jewel was sent here in the first place. What is the relation between the new king of Meridian and this world? I always said it was a waste of time."

Arkon replied, "That is my opinion too."

She turned to him and said, "Arkon." Then she walked to him and hugged him. "I'm sorry!" Arkon didn't talk at all, then she said, "I have a filming session. I will leave." She got in her new car and started to drive away, then she stopped and added, "I don't like your clothes!" Then she left.

In the meantime, Arya replaced the phone that Caleb destroyed, only to realize that she doesn't know anyone's number. Arkon called her to demand that she bring his car because he has somewhere to go. He was annoyed when she refused to let him drive himself, so he asked how to obtain a license. He took Arya to the location where he thought Tynar lost his coordinates, which just happened to be the same place where Arya buried the diamond ring from Caleb. Arya asked what the coordinates looked like, but Arkon said she wouldn't be able to see them.

A few minutes across, Arkon decided to stop searching for the magical map and sat beside Arya. She looked at him and said, "Shall we take a photo to save this memory?"

Arkon stared at her and replied, "Consider it a great honor." But when she couldn't get both of their faces in the shot, Arkon snatched the phone away and pulled her in close.

He turned his head to find her very close, and they both froze. Arkon heard voices like a mermaid's song in his head. Then he said, "Meridian!" He felt something strange. He sensed the Jewel of Meridian. Then he concentrated, and he thought he was affected by the close proximity. Arkon gulped a few times, then counted down for the picture.

Hilariously, they couldn't manage to take a single picture where both of them had their eyes open. It broke the tension, and even when they finally got a shot with their eyes open, they were both making weird faces. Arkon gave up, and Arya sent him the pictures, and he cracked a tiny smile as he flipped through the silly photos.

While they were walking, she asked, "Will everything end when you find the magical stones and the jewel?"

Arkon replied, "Yes."

Then she asked, "Will you leave then?"

"Yes."

Arya stared at him, then said, "I think your word to protect me was temporary."

"What?" Arkon asked.

"Nothing! But what if you come back and you haven't gained your powers back?"

"That will not happen; I'm Meridian, and Meridian is me," Arkon replied.

Then Arya said, "Oh, that's comfy. In the beginning, when Cornelia and Caleb refused to give you the stones, I thought it's a conspiracy because I didn't know that they lost the stones." Arkon wondered, *A conspiracy?*

Arya replied, "Yes, I think you don't have things like these in your world."

Arkon replied, "No, we don't. I was born to be a king. Things are different in the world of immortals." He added, "I heard that people choose their own kings in this world." Arya said that there are no more kings, just people entrusted with authority for a temporary term.

She explained that the problem is when they elect people who forget that, so they have to be sure to elect people with good memories. She said, "It doesn't matter because I'm going to leave for another place."

Arkon asked, "Does it really not matter?"

Arya said, "What?"

Arkon replied, "What if I'm forced to leave Meridian forever? What if I couldn't come back there? Would I feel it like you said? I don't know, but that will not happen because I can't imagine my world without me."

They drove the car to Tynar's workplace. They picked up Tynar after work, and Arya asked them to direct her to Caleb's penthouse so she could retrieve the land contract. Arkon said that he needs to go to the land of the gate, insisting that his need is greater than hers. Tynar quietly suggested that they eat something, and Arkon's growling stomach settled the argument to his chagrin.

Before they went, Nani called Arya, "Arya, come to my booth because there's someone here you need to meet."

Nani glowered at Arkon and asked Arya why Arkon was still hanging around. She pulled Arya aside to say that she met a magical man and that he was here to meet Arya. She dragged Arya into her weird little fortune-telling booth, where a shadow lurked behind a beaded curtain. Arya impatiently got up to leave, then stopped dead in her tracks when the man said, "You have no luck with your parents."

He clucked his tongue and said that she was frustrated because of her land, which was both hers and not hers. He said that it's not in her fate to sell the land because a heavy spirit is driving away all of her luck. The man claimed that a dark creature was living in her house and that things would worsen unless she kicked him out! Arya whispered that he's not a dark creature, but he is an immortal, and the man barked that a dark creature wouldn't admit he was dark. Suddenly, from behind Arya, Arkon's voice deadpanned: "Whom are you calling a dark creature?"

The man parted the beads, and Arkon saw Herbert, the banished magical servant who made terrible things and left Meridian to live in the human world. Herbert shoved Arya into Arkon and made a run for it. Arkon was hot on his heels, with Tynar not far behind. Herbert headed for the stairwell, nearly colliding with Nani, who windmilled dangerously before Tynar caught her in his arms. It was adorably romantic…until Tynar gently left Nani on the floor and resumed the chase, leaving her with her toes still pointed skyward.

Arkon nearly caught Herbert several times as he fled the building and took off down the street, but he was thwarted every time. Eventually, Herbert found his way to a balcony and jumped to the ground below. Arkon made a leap worthy of a superhero, staying just behind him as Herbert entered another building and climbed to the roof.

Just as Arkon caught up, Herbert jumped off the building, falling a frightening distance. Arkon looked over the edge, but all he saw was Tynar standing next to a Herbert-shaped impression in the concrete, and Herbert wasn't there!

After this futile chase, Arya took Tynar and Arkon to the restaurant to eat. Then she asked, "Why were you trying to catch him?"

Arkon replied, "He was doing bad things back in Meridian, but he was banished. I didn't want to hurt him, but when he first saw me, he ran. That means he did something wrong for someone close to me. Or something bad in general."

Arya asked, "Is there a way to break my family's curse?" Arkon said it's not a curse but a promise her family made for committing a sin. She insisted that he tell her what sin was committed to understanding, so he slammed down his fork and complied.

"Long ago, thousands of years ago, there was a woman attacked and thrown into the water, and the rules were broken so she could live in Meridian. She lived a good life, but one day she became ill with worry over her blind mother, so she was sent back home. She was sent back to earth. She fell in love with the king in her own country and got married, and never returned to Meridian. The entire realm of immortals felt betrayed after all that they'd done for her."

Arkon grew more and more furious as he recited the story, and when Arya asked if her name was Tylen, he stormed out of the restaurant.

Arya got their food packed up and rejoined Arkon and Tynar in the car.

Arya said, "I want to go and see Caleb now."

Arkon replied, "There's no need to meet him." Then he handed her a stack of shredded paper.

She said, "It's the land's sale contract."

Arkon said, "How dare you sell the land of the gate! I was shocked when I read the contract. I don't know why you want to sell the land, but forget it; the land will not be sold, so don't waste your time."

Arya started to cry and sobbed, "Why are you doing this to me? What did I do to deserve that? This contract was fundamental to me."

She got out of the car and walked away. Arkon was surprised by her emotional reaction. His anger dissipated, and he followed her. He grabbed her wrist to stop her, and she said that she was happy when he said he'd protect her because she thought she finally had someone on her side.

Arya started to cry hard as she continued to say that she knew his time here was short but that she liked being happy, even if it was foolish and temporary. But now she shook her head at Arkon, saying that she doesn't know what kind of king he is.

Arkon said haughtily that he's the next king of Meridian, and Arya agreed that he's someone from a world bigger than hers and meant to do bigger things. She said that it wouldn't matter if small, nameless things left without a trace. It broke her heart. She was referring to herself.

Pulling her arm from his grasp, Arya walked away from Arkon, leaving him looking shaken. She wiped her tears and called Julian to ask if she could visit him at home. She hung up and continued walking, and as she crossed the street, a truck swerved around a broken-down vehicle and barreled toward her. Arkon barely had time to call a warning before the truck slammed right into Arya. He ran to the spot where she was just standing, but she was gone without a trace. Gasping in panic, Arkon screamed, "Arya! Arya!"

Chapter Seven
I Exposed You

Arkon said, "She's gone." He looked around frantically and crossed the street. He saw Caleb smirking with an unconscious Arya in his arms. She woke, and Caleb carefully set her down. Arkon managed to stay calm as he asked what happened, and Caleb said he had been following them all day. He asked Arya if they fought, but she walked away from both of them and got into a taxi without saying a word.

The taxi driver was an old man with totally white hair. He asked, "Why do you look concerned?"

Arya replied, "There is nothing."

The man said, "You seem like you just faced death!" Arya raised her head, then he continued, "There was a customer before you who said that he was about to die four times this month, and he finally accepted his destiny to live in peace."

Arya replied, "If this was his destiny, it's better for him to think in that way."

The man replied, "I don't think that you know what destiny is. The half of the fate is the part that is connected with your lifetime, and you can't change that half, but the other half of the fate is the part that changes with your ways to handle it; what I mean is that you can change your destiny!" Arya was surprised by what she heard from the taxi driver. She looked at his hand and was shocked to see the ring with the tree sign on it. She thought about where she had seen this ring before, and then she knew it was from the librarian. She wondered, *Is this a coincidence?*

The driver continued, "When you come to life, it's all about how you handle it. It's like car driving when you choose a good and expert driver. You will get to your destination safely, like now!" Arya looked around and saw that she had arrived at Julian's address. She couldn't believe how fast she had arrived there.

She arrived at a giant garden with high walls; she entered through the big iron door and wondered what a businessman like Julian was doing here! She found Julian pruning trees. She handed him the land sale contract, which she had taped back together as best she could. With an offhand comment that someone must not want her to sell, Julian offered to reprint the contract, and when Arya insisted on signing now, he said he didn't have the company's seal with him.

Arya was very disappointed, then apologized to him and turned to leave. But Julian stopped her and said, "Are you kidding me?"

Arya replied, "Sorry?"

Julian said, "You have come this far, and you think I will let you go like this?" Arya ended up helping him prune trees. As they work, he said, "Hard labor helps get the mind off of problems."

When Arya marveled that he has a hobby like this, Julian said that he may seem cold, but he's actually a very sentimental person! Arya agreed that he comes across as closed-off, and she asked how he became a successful businessman. Julian said that he could read people's emotions if he tried hard enough.

Arya quipped that there are lots of people around her who can do that sort of thing. One of them ran like the wind and created diamonds from nothing, and another becomes an expert at something after only seeing it done once. Julian just smiled. He seemed to believe that was not just a joke. Arya asked, "Why do you spend your free time taking care of trees?" He said that trees live a long time and that they create forests but still coexist peacefully with other living things and even provide for them when needed.

He asked if tiring herself out made her forget her problems. Then he asked what upset her. She said that she feels strangely compelled to unload herself to him. He said that it's just because he's another person, and he told her to think she's talking to a tree.

Arya stared at him and said, "I made a mistake that a lot of people make. I depended on someone without realizing that, and I made expectations, and the most important thing was that I exposed my feelings about the worst thing that bothers me."

Julian asked, "Did you think that he's the proper person to do that with?"

Arya replied, "No, I knew he was not the proper person. I don't know why I did that. He will leave soon anyway." Then she lowered her voice and said, "To be specific, he is not a person!"

Julian said compassionately, "This person sounds like a bad person if he knows he is leaving and messed with your heart anyway."

Meanwhile, Arkon kept watching for Arya from his rooftop until after dark, waiting for her to come back.

Julian drove Arya home, and she apologized for misjudging him, which made him really happy. He drove off with a satisfied smile.

As Arya neared her house, she braced herself, unsure if she'd see Arkon waiting for her in his usual spot under the yellow streetlight. When she rounded a corner and saw him there, she reminded herself of Julian's words that a person who's leaving but still messes with her heart isn't a good person. But still, she stopped to talk to him and asked what he was doing. He answered, "I'm thinking of a way to regain my powers."

Arya asked, "Did you go to the land of the gate? My land!"

Arkon answered, "No!"

Arya was surprised and said, "Why? You wanted to go badly. What happened?" He explained that he doesn't have a driver's license and didn't trust Caleb enough to ask for a ride.

When Arya smiled, Arkon asked, "Does this mean that we made up from our fight?"

Arya asserted, "Everything I said today was a lie about being disappointed in you. Humans lie when they're angry. Please forget what I said earlier today."

Arkon replied, "I knew you were lying because it's obvious when you do." She walked inside the house, and he went to the rooftop. Arya opened the table lamp and sat next to it, thinking of Arkon. He did the same thing in his place. They stayed up late that night, troubled…

In the meantime, on a beach, Cornelia crouched by the water's edge, looking at the weak and dying fish that were washing up onto the sand. Caleb called her and asked, "Where are you?"

She replied, "I'm working on something because I'm the only one who is suffering here. I can't afford more energy to help this world. Humans will never change; the water is contaminated. The water creatures are dying."

"Stop complaining and listen to me. Do you know what I did the whole day?" Caleb asked.

Cornelia replied, "Why would I know?"

"Believe me. You want to know because I followed Arkon the whole day."

She replied, "Don't furl my jealousy. Just do your job."

"I saw Herbert!" Caleb said.

"What? Where are you now?" she asked.

"I'm beside the pool," Caleb replied. She immediately hung up, disappeared from the beach, and appeared next to him beside the pool. He looked at her and said, "I really know how to bring you here."

"What happened? Does Arkon know everything now? Tell me," Cornelia asked.

He smiled and said, "Herbert is awful. He ran away like a rat." She breathed a sigh of relief. Caleb asked, "Does that really make you nervous?"

She stared and said, "You must find Van. We must put everything into the normal situation."

The following day, Arya woke up to her ringing phone. She picked it up, and it was Julian. He told Arya that he had created a new contract, and they agreed to meet at night to sign it.

Arya was startled to find Arkon on her couch. He waved her keys when she asked how he got in, saying that she left them at the door last night. Arkon asked, "Did you sell the land?" Arya felt guilty when he asked her.

She replied, "Not yet."

"Will you sell it because you need money?"

"Yes, actually. I wouldn't sell the land if everything were good," Arya replied.

"Okay, then sell it. You can do whatever you want!" Arkon said.

Arya was surprised and quaked, "Sorry!"

"You said the money would help you, so you can sell it," he replied. Then he walked and turned to her. "By the way, whom were you calling?"

He narrowed his eyes and asked again whom she was just talking to on the phone. Suspicious, Arkon stalked towards Arya, backing her all the way to the wall. He leaned close, barely inches from her face, and her cheeks went red. He noted her blush and racing heart, then announced triumphantly, "It was a man." He walked away, and Arya's knees gave out. She sank to the floor, wondering what just happened. Arkon stomped up to the roof and started to strip for a bath. Arya followed and got a start at the sight of his shirtless torso. Then she was distracted by the expensive clothes that Tynar had hung up. Tynar explained that Cornelia sent them.

In the meantime, the beauty goddess Cornelia fended off an ardent lover, dramatically telling him to leave and never look for her again. He started to cry, and leaned forward to kiss her; then he suddenly started to shake and gasp for air. Cornelia sighed and told him to breathe, but he crashed to the ground, unconscious. Cornelia rolled her eyes and walked away…from the scene they were filming. But the man's distress was real, and this happened to all of her leading men whenever they tried to film a kiss scene. Everyone rushed to him as Cornelia headed to her dressing room.

Caleb entered and sent everyone away. He giggled when he heard that another of Cornelia's co-stars was sent to the hospital. He tagged along as she visited Julian in his office, gloating that he and Cornelia have the kind of friendship where they trust each other with their lives. Julian wondered what people do to forge such a strong bond. She told Julian that she was looking to leave the resort because she had bought another apartment. Julian replied, "Oh, that's unfortunate. Our resort became famous after you lived here for a while, but don't worry. I understand your request."

Cornelia replied, "Thank you, and I'm sorry because I'm suddenly leaving."

She left with Caleb. Back in her suite, Caleb said that he had never heard Cornelia apologize before. She replied that Julian is a decent person, strong against the strong and weak against the weak. Caleb marveled sarcastically at her ability to read people, and Cornelia sneered that he knew nothing about her. Then she got a call from Arkon, who said that he was on his way over. He mentioned Caleb but said that he doesn't trust him. After he hung up, Tynar asked why he was not telling Arya about this, and Arkon revealed that he didn't want her to be involved.

Caleb asked, "Where are you going?"

Cornelia replied, "You can't come; I will go alone, and you must go now."

"If you will continue doing that, maybe I will transform into my evil version!" Caleb replied.

"I don't care; do what you want," Cornelia said. He stared at her angrily and left.

The three, Cornelia, Arkon, and Tynar, went to Arya's land, the land of the magical gate. Cornelia said, "This is the first time I have come here after that day."

Arkon asked her, "Didn't you say that Van had asked you to come here that day because he saw something suspicious?"

Cornelia answered, "Yes, that's true." Arkon remembered when he came here for the first time when he came to this world; he remembered the stone with blood, then he walked toward the location of the rock, but Cornelia commented that Van went in another direction when they were here the last time many years ago.

Arkon came close, leaned, and zeroed in on a rock that was stained by blood.

He lifted the stone, then Tynar and Cornelia saw it; they were really surprised to see it. Arkon said, "I didn't care when I saw it the first time, but when I heard what Van said to you, that there was something strange here, I came to make sure. What do you think this is?" Cornelia hesitated, then Arkon spoke. "This is blood!" She took two steps forward, then Arkon gave her the stone with the blood and said, "Sense it."

She put it in her hand and asserted, "Yes, I sense human blood, but how? That is impossible! There is nothing that can leave a trace on this land; it's magical."

"I know this land is purging itself of any human trace," Arkon said. He continued, "It must be from Meridian, but the question is, how? There is no one there who has blood, so what is that?"

In the meantime, Julian was planting flowers on his farm with the help of an adorable little blind girl. They finished up, and the little girl said that her grandmother invited Julian over to eat. He wilted dramatically and pouted that he had an important meeting; then he took a few steps away when his phone rang.

The little girl called out to him, wailing that there was a bug on her arm. Julian's eyes flashed, and he rushed back to flick away the caterpillar on the girl's wrist. He hugged her tightly and told her it was okay, then led her away. Behind them, the caterpillar burst into flame!

On the drive back to the city, Cornelia asked, "Do you think that Van's disappearance is related to the blood on the rock?"

Arkon sighed and said, "It's weird, but I think so."

Cornelia replied, "Maybe the magical servants know something about that because there is a really big count of them in this world. They came here through the years when your father decided to create the veil; he prevented the humans from discovering the other worlds, including the world of Meridian, but he didn't prevent the creatures from coming from our world, so that caused a lot of chaos. Will we hide this from Caleb?"

Arkon replied, "Don't tell him now."

She said, "I don't trust him very much, but he still knows about the magical servants' locations. I think he can help; I know you hated him since he convinced Queen Wera to make the servants' strain a thousand years ago, but he was born like that; we can't change him."

She looked at him and asked, "Do you really want to find Van quickly?"

Arkon replied, "What do you mean?"

She answered, "Caleb said that you don't want to leave fast!" Arkon stared at her and spoke no word. Then she pulled over beside the beach coast, and they got out to talk. Cornelia said, "Caleb was uttering silly things, right? If you want to lie, keep your mouth close." She walked to the edge and flew close to him, then she turned her back against the water and her face toward Arkon and said, "You know that I always lie to you, but in thousands of years, you didn't speak even one single lie, but sometimes I hope you lie to me. Do you know why? Because I know how your words are important to all of us. I don't want to believe what Caleb said." She got serious and nervous, then she continued, "I don't want you to make the same fault again. I don't want you to love another human girl."

He wanted to explode, but he kept calm and said, "What are you talking about?"

Cornelia kneeled at Arkon's feet and said that she'd submit if he wanted to punish her for her impertinence.

Arkon said, "Let's go."

A few hours later, in a classy restaurant, Arya met with Julian to sign the land sale contract. She hesitated first, remembering Arkon saying that she can sell anything she wants but the gate land, but then she recalled him telling her to do whatever she wants. As Julian was watching, she decisively stamped the papers. They have dinner to celebrate, and when Julian asked if she was sad to sell her family's land, Arya replied that it was just useless land. He asked what her parents thought, and she told him that her father had left and her mother had passed away. She said flippantly that Julian wouldn't understand, being from a rich family, but he informed her that he's an orphan. He said that he never knew his mother and that his father was abusive and abandoned him. Arya dropped her fork in surprise and reached for it, but Julian took her hand and told her to leave the fork. He asked the waiter to bring a new one.

In the meantime, in the car, Cornelia asked if anyone felt hungry because there were a lot of good restaurants here. Tynar nodded immediately, but Arkon said, "No, I don't want to eat."

Suddenly, Cornelia stopped the car and asked, "Do you know this woman?"

They turned to the window, and Tynar said, "It's Arya! Who is that man? I'm sure I've seen him before."

Cornelia said, "It's Mr. Julian. He's the owner of the resort that I was living at. I didn't know that he knew this woman."

Tynar continued, "Oh, yes, this man is her rich friend. I didn't know that he had buildings."

Arkon ordered, "Move." Cornelia turned to him and saw his eyes filled with tension.

Julian apologized to Arya for being so blunt about his family and disturbing the atmosphere at dinner. He offered her a ride home, but she declined since it was such a nice evening to walk. He said he had a question since she mentioned the night air. "How fast was the breeze that shook your heart?"

She froze because she didn't know what to say, then she said, "Good night." And left.

She walked to her home, thinking about what Julian just said. She thought, *He's a very good man, handsome, rich, and gentle. Oh my god, I don't know what I'm thinking of!* She approached the street's corner before her house and thought that she would find Arkon waiting for her in the usual spot, under the yellow streetlight, but she felt disappointed because he wasn't there. She walked the rest of the way alone. She opened the iron gate and crept to the roof to look around, and she was startled to see Arkon sitting alone in the dark.

Arkon said, "What are you doing here?"

Arya replied, "I saw the lights off, so I wanted to check out if you were here."

"You can take a rest because I want to be alone!" Arkon stated.

Arya replied, "Oh, yes." She walked two steps, then she said, "I wanted to ask you that sometimes when I came at night, you were standing down the street—"

Arkon interrupted her and said, "I will not do that anymore! However, it's not a long time before I will go back to Meridian." Arya nodded and left him alone. He looked down at the bloody rock in his hand, remembering Cornelia saying that nobody from the realm of the immortals has any blood. He called her to ask if the magical servants might know any old legends. Cornelia asked, "What legend?"

Arkon replied, "This blood." He growled. "I have an idea of whose it is."

Arya went to her bed, hugging her signed contract and dreaming of her dream—that she would sell everything here and move to live on an island. But she couldn't fall asleep, so she knocked on the little door leading to Arkon's room on the rooftop, and when he didn't answer, she opened the door. She freaked out because Arkon was standing behind the door. She asked, "Why didn't you answer me?"

Arkon replied, "What do you want?"

"I want to ask you about something because I'm feeling bad," Arya replied.

"What?" Arkon asked.

"So, why can't I sell my family's land? The magical gate will stay there even if the owner changes, so why can't I sell it?" Arya replied.

Arkon replied, "I told you that you can do whatever you want with it."

"I know, but I want to know the reason, please," Arya replied.

Arkon's facial expressions changed, and he spoke. "Well, they will criticize me because I couldn't save the gate land."

Arya was surprised and said, "I thought that was not important because you are a prince and you will be the next king of your world."

Arkon replied, "Even in our world, there are people who use these opportunities against the rulers."

That stopped Arya short, and she went to bed, reassuring herself that she shouldn't be expected to sacrifice for something that may not even happen. But Arkon's words haunted her all night, and she woke up with panda eyes from lost sleep. Arya woke up, and she immediately thought about an excuse to go to the rooftop and see Arkon. She took the laundry upstairs, and Tynar helped her hang up the laundry, and she asked him if he was hungry, but he chirped that they were going to eat with Cornelia. He said that they saw her with Julian last night, teasing that they look good together, and Arkon, who was sitting under a sunny spot reading, slammed his book close, then stomped off.

Arya watched him go, wondering if seeing her with Julian meant that Arkon knew she was selling the land. She told herself that Arkon doesn't know who the potential buyer is, then remembered that he saw the contract, working herself into a tizzy.

In the meantime, Caleb and Cornelia were sitting in Caleb's penthouse. Cornelia asked, "Do you know a magical servant that lived very long?"

Caleb stared at her and said, "Yes, I think so."

Cornelia asked, "Who?"

Caleb smiled and said, "You know him too! It's Herbert."

Not far away, a line of fancy cars was parked outside an abandoned warehouse. It was the meeting of the magical servants, who needled each other about their dealings with humans before sitting down to a lavish meal. Herbert joined them, and he learned that Van was missing and that the guardians had asked the magical servants to find him. The servants called Herbert a hero for being the only one who escaped from Arkon, but he stammered that they shouldn't talk about the future king that way. One of the servants took offense, yelling that he came here to get away from that jerk Arkon. Suddenly, the doors to the warehouse swung open, and Caleb walked in.

When they first saw Caleb, they started to run. They all left the place. When Herbert approached the door, Caleb waved his hand, and the door closed on Herbert's face. Caleb approached him slowly, and Herbert was terrified. Then he was utterly terrified to see Cornelia and her blonde hair waving in the air, looking every inch the vengeful immortal. She made him explain why he saw Arkon then ran away, and he spluttered that he didn't say anything to Arkon.

Cornelia ordered him to shut his mouth, and he squeaked that, of course, he didn't say it was her! Caleb was amused at how Cornelia was losing control of the conversation. Herbert continued that he definitely didn't tell Arkon that Cornelia told him to hit him! And she screamed at him to shut his mouth.

A few minutes later, Caleb deposited an unconscious Herbert into Cornelia's car. She snapped at Caleb for laughing, and he asked if she was afraid Arkon would discover she was jealous!

He caught Cornelia's expression and seemed to realize he'd gone too far. He told Cornelia seriously just to confess her feelings toward Arkon and get rejected because he hated seeing her like this. He blustered, saying that it was not appropriate behavior for the most beautiful and powerful creature on this planet.

In the meantime, Arkon and Tynar were waiting for Cornelia. Over lunch, Arkon told Tynar that Queen Wera in Meridian once told him a story that he thought was nonsense. But if Herbert was as old as Queen Wera, then he might know something that could help Arkon find who left the blood on the rock!

Cornelia called Arkon, and he headed to her place. Herbert started groveling as soon as he saw Arkon, and Cornelia said to him, "If you answer our question, we'll let you go, but if you ever talk about it, I will freeze your tongue and smash it."

Arkon showed Herbert the bloody rock and told him where he found it. Herbert knew it was not possible, saying there was only one person who could make human blood show up at the magical gate. Both Arkon and Cornelia knew precisely who he meant, though nobody had ever seen him before!

Later in the hotel restaurant, Cornelia said that Caleb talked about that person a lot, too. They were interrupted by Julian, who approached their table amicably, but Arkon just glared at him. Cornelia told Julian that they saw him and Arya last night. Julian asked, "Are you the patient who I saw with Arya last time?" Cornelia laughed when she heard Julian refer to Arkon as a patient. Julian stretched his hand to shake Arkon's hand, but Arkon stared directly into Julian's eyes and ignored his hand.

Cornelia said that if she were human, she would fall in love with Julian. She added that he was too good for Arya but figured she could push them together anyway, then tried to steer the conversation back to another subject because she noticed Arkon's facial expressions had changed.

But Arkon was no longer listening as he continued to stare at Julian, who found Arya standing in the entryway. Arya said that she was there to find someone, and Julian told her affably that if she keeps being this nervous, he'll think she changed her mind about selling the land. She looked confused, so Julian said, "I just got rejected, didn't I?" But he was smiling.

At their table, Cornelia said, "I have never seen Julian smile like that before." Arkon had seen enough, and he got up and stalked over to Julian.

Arya tried to take Julian and escape, but Arkon cut them off, holding up a silencing hand. He leaned close to whisper in Julian's ear, "I have caught on to you."

Julian's eyes flew open, and he looked at Arkon in horror. With a triumphant sneer, Arkon repeated himself, "I said, 'I have caught on to you'."

Chapter Eight
The Magical Stones

Two thousand eight hundred fifty years ago, in a dank, dark cave in Meridian, a young child in filthy rags picked up a dead leaf. He took a bite out of it, then shoved the whole thing in his mouth. He scooped up a whole pile of leaves and ran back into the safety of the cave.

In the realm of the Meridian, Arkon had been studying how humans make more humans. He asked the high priest how immortals were made, those who are not made from the marriage of two immortals since they don't all marry.

Coughing, the high priest said, "These kinds of immortals just came into existence, but nobody knows who created them." Arkon complained that was too ambiguous, but the high priest said that it's the humans' matter to try to make sense of things and the world around them, but immortals are just immortals.

Arkon walked with the high priest through a waterfall portal, where they found Cornelia and Caleb waiting for them. The high priest continued that some immortal have borne children by borrowing the bodies of humans, resulting in a being that is both human and immortals and has an eternal life.

Cornelia and Caleb found the idea abhorrent, but the high priest told them that such a creature does exist! The child of a human woman and a male immortal. He said that such children aren't immortal because they grow and change like humans, but they aren't human because they have immortal powers. "They are an existence that either immortals or humans do not welcome."

Arkon asked, "I want to ask you something. Is he using his powers for good?"

The high priest sighed and said, "The powers we have are seeking to give life and care about everything in life, but this creature's power is the opposite." He walked two steps, then turned and said, "His power is destroying. These half-immortals' powers are destructive since their divine element is fire!"

Caleb asked if that made this creature stronger than Arkon, and he looked excited by the idea, but Cornelia protested that it's not possible. The high priest said he didn't know, then Cornelia and Caleb stormed off, bickering as usual.

The high priest reassured Arkon that it couldn't be true since he was fated to be king. But Arkon didn't look convinced.

Arkon asked the high priest if half-immortals were good or evil, and the high priest said that it depended on how they used their powers. If they use them for good, they're good, and if they use them for evil, they're evil. Or if they use them for strange purposes, it means they're strange.

Later, the three young immortals discuss the matter. Caleb thought that when the high priest said he didn't know whether half-immortals were stronger than Arkon, it was as good as admitting that it was true. Cornelia reminded him that it meant they'd be stronger than *him*, too. She told Arkon to avoid these creatures if he ever ran into one.

Arkon denied being scared since, as an immortal, he has eternal life. Cornelia told Arkon not to worry too much about half-immortals since they live in hiding, and he would recognize them the moment he saw one.

PRESENT

After Arkon whispered in Julian's ears, Julian hardly controlled his nerves. He said, "I don't know what you are talking about."

He wanted to leave, but Arkon said in a louder voice, "You are growing old like your human mother, but you don't die like your immortal father!" Arkon showed Julian the bloody rock from the magical gate, snarling, "This is your blood, isn't it?" Unable to hide his reaction anymore, Julian began to shake, but Arya interrupted and tried to pull Arkon away. He asked Arya, "Do you know his true identity?"

She said, "He's the CEO of the resort." Cornelia arrived to apologize for Arkon's behavior, giving Julian a chance to escape.

Arkon ordered Cornelia to stay near Caleb while he wanted to check something. He stared angrily at Arya, who indeed had no idea what was going on.

Julian went to his office and looked at all of his photos and awards, signifying years of trying to pass as human. He realized that when Arya said a few days ago that she knew people with powers, she wasn't just joking around, and he started to sweat nervously as he realized that she was talking about Arkon. He looked angry as he thought to himself, *Arya...*

In the meantime, as Arya drove away, she wondered what Arkon meant about Julian's true identity. Meanwhile, Arkon, Cornelia, and Caleb sat together in Caleb's penthouse. Arkon said, "You were right, Cornelia, when you told me thousands of years ago about this creature. I knew that Julian was a half-immortal at a single glance."

Cornelia replied, "But...I can't believe that Mr. Julian is a half-human and half immortal!"

Tynar uttered, "Does that mean he is stronger than Prince Arkon?"

Cornelia hit him on the head; then she yelled at Arkon, "Why did you do that? I told you thousands of years ago, before we became the guards. I told you, if you meet that creature someday, don't face him. You are powerless now. What if he was planning for something evil? What if he hits you? Did you lose your mind like your powers?"

Arkon replied, "I wanted him to expose himself." He silenced, then he said, "He must have a hand in Van's disappearance." Meanwhile, Caleb was keeping his anger inside him. He had something against this creature. Arkon asked Caleb to drive him home.

In the car, Caleb said, "You have no evidence that he is half immortal except for your sense."

Arkon replied, "Staying all this time in the human world made you one of them!"

"I must think like humans. Even in Meridian, when we were together, you and Cornelia made me feel like I'm less than you because you were stronger," Caleb replied.

Caleb insisted that they need to confirm Julian's identity; then he sighed at the coincidence that he was close to Arya. He offered to find out how they met and about their relationship, but Arkon ordered him to leave Arya out of this. Caleb argued that the immortals' servant belonged to all of them, so he needed to protect what was theirs. When he dropped Arkon off, Caleb called after him, saying that it was Arkon who dragged humans back into all of this. He said that even if Arya is a loyal servant who doesn't go to Julian's side, Julian is probably curious about Arya's relationship with Arkon and will use her for his sake. Caleb said that Julian might even feel entitled to use the immortals' servant, too. But he added in a snarky tone that his senses have dulled from being in the human world, so he'll let Arkon handle it alone.

In the meantime, Arya was still worried about Arkon's reaction when he would find out she sold the land. Arya tried to tell herself that it was her land to do with as she pleased. But she couldn't stop thinking about Arkon, saying that he'd be thought of as the king who couldn't protect his land. A sudden clap of thunder startled her.

It was Caleb, snapping his fingers and creating lightning in a fit of temper. Cornelia called him to yell at him to knock it off, but he said it was his warning to that half-immortal. He had a wave of great anger inside him, and the weather changed from sunny to cloudy because of his powers.

Arkon went to Arya's clinic, waiting for her to come. He was trying to ignore Matt's whining about him being there. Matt approached Arkon, who was sitting on the chair, and said, "Well, I don't want to bother you or something, but you are only Arya's neighbor; you can't come here whenever you want without an appointment. If you have something, you can tell her when she comes back to her house." He went silent, then he said, "No, actually, you can't see her even in the alley."

Arkon opened his eyes widely and said, "Nurse Matt, if you will keep talking thinking that my patience won't run out, you are wrong."

"However, I just wanted to explain that you can't be close to Arya. She allowed you to stay at her place because she has a kind heart, so don't expect more than that. Also, she has a boyfriend. He is wealthy, and he loves her very much." Arkon controlled his nerves hardly, knowing that Matt was lying.

In the meantime, the reception door opened, and Arya entered when she first saw Arkon. She uttered, "Oh my God." She asked, "What are you doing here?"

But Arkon didn't answer; they entered her office, and Matt brought them two cups of coffee, and he put the cracked cup in front of Arkon. Arya pointed to Matt to leave; then she switched the cups and said, "They say that drinking in a cracked cup brings bad luck, but my luck will not be worse."

She asked again, "Why have you come here?"

Arkon replied, "I came because I want to accompany you when you go home!" Arya spat the coffee immediately, and her cheeks became red.

After finishing her work, Arya and Arkon walked home at night. Arkon said, "The weather is so fine, but I didn't mean that we literally walk. I meant we go in my car that Cornelia gave me."

"Well, Matt asked me to take the car; he wanted to show it to his friends, so I couldn't say no to him," Arya replied.

Arkon asked if she really has a boyfriend. He looked it up on the internet and discovered that it would mean Arya was dating someone. He segued into asking if Arya has such a relationship with Julian, and she stammered that, of course, it's not like that.

She stopped, turned, then said, "I will take you to wonderful places today, and I will buy you nice clothes! Consider it an early farewell gift to you."

She took Arkon to an amusement park, where everything terrified him. He screamed so loudly in the haunted house that he frightened the actors playing ghosts. Then he insisted on riding the roller coaster over and over to conquer his fear. Arya ended up dragging him off the ride, literally, and when he muttered that it's not right for a servant to push her king around, she fired back that it's not right for a king to put his life in danger for silly things. Arkon called her cute, which flustered her, though she definitely liked it.

Arya said, "I think I'm too old to hear this word!"

Arkon replied, "I'm older than 4000 years!" Then she got the point. Arkon stood and said, "Let's go. I feel like a joker here." They walked out of the park. Arkon asked, "Why do you want to go and live on an island? When I arrived on this planet, the gate was opened in a different country. It was on some island called Princess Island; it was an extraordinary place, and then I came here by another gate. I understand that living in a beautiful place like that is your wish, but I want to know why."

"Well, I wonder if being there will make me feel better. When some problems are too hard to solve, I always want to leave the place with all its problems," Arya replied.

Arkon asked, "Is that because of what you call money?"

Arya said, "Yes, you can say it's one of the problems. Also, because of my father, I want to have a fresh start."

She stopped and stared at him, then she said, "I want to ask you about what you said earlier to Mr. Julian." Arkon said that he told Julian not to make moves on his woman! But the way he said it was a bit vague, so Arya was unsure if he was being romantic or just possessive of his servant.

Neither of them noticed that Julian was watching them from a short distance away. He recalled Arya saying that she made the mistake of relying on someone she shouldn't have because he's going to leave; she'd added that that 'person' isn't really a person, and Julian connected the dots. Julian said, "Is he what she meant that day?"

The next morning, Arkon woke just in time to see Arya leaving for work. He thought about Arya saying that he was someone with important things to do, so it didn't matter to him if lesser beings disappeared. So he called her to invite her to go home together again when she was off work. Then he ended the call.

In the meantime, Chairman Hale rejected yet another of Miranda's get-famous-quick schemes when he realized it meant she'd be modeling in skimpy bikinis. He ordered her to forget becoming a Hollywood star and go to work at Julian's Block World shopping mall. Suddenly, Miranda realized that Julian was the one trying to buy Chairman Hale's land, and she shocked her grandfather by agreeing to handle the sale. It was mostly an excuse to talk to Julian, who was distracted and completely ignored her when she went to see him. She touched his arm, and he jerked away violently, saying he was too busy to talk.

She turned to Secretary Nigel, who pretended he didn't see her, so she chased him down to ask what was wrong with Julian. Miranda said she was here because she was in charge of the land sale now, but Secretary Nigel replied, "The hard part is done, and all we have to do is sign the contract."

She changed the subject and asked, "Have you noticed Julian's weird behavior lately? Don't misunderstand me; I'm not asking about him because I like him or something, but I'm only curious."

"No, actually, you like him because you act exactly like the high school girls at the church who come to ask me for love advice."

When Arya arrived at her office in the clinic, Matt spotted the amusement park tickets sticking out of her wallet. He asked whom she went with. She refused to discuss it, so he snapped that it better not be Arkon. After he left, Arya mooned over the tickets, remembering Arkon calling her his woman. Her cheeks became red, so she slapped her face lightly and went out of the office to inhale the fresh air, but she was surprised to see Julian in front of the office room.

Arya and Julian sat in her office as a doctor and her patient. He asked for a psychiatric evaluation, citing a sleep disorder that he blamed on his personal past.

With difficulty, he admitted that he never knew his mother and that his father treated him as if he were a monster. He'd named him 'disgrace' and kept him locked up for fear others would find out about his existence. Julian's voice hitched as he said that one cold winter night, his father cast him out.

FLASHBACK – JULIAN'S CHILDHOOD

In the dark and cold, a boy flew out the magical gate in Arya's family land. The clouds were covering the moon and the stars. It was the same boy who was trapped in the cave in Meridian. Young Julian bled from the mouth, and some of the blood dripped onto a stone just outside the portal. Then this boy ran toward the woods.

END OF FLASHBACK

Julian said while he remembered, "On that night, I didn't fear the dark because I was used to it, but I was afraid of the unfamiliar air. I faced the world for the first time; it smelled, and the scene was quite different from the place I was trapped in." The silence took hold; then Julian continued.

"Until this moment, I didn't know where this place was, and I don't want to know. I was scared, and I wanted only to leave. Then in the woods, a light flashed once, then twice, so I ran toward the light…" He stopped and focused on Arya's facial expressions.

He thought, *She feels sympathy; she doesn't show any marks of hate or contempt; she is definitely not one of them. If she knew who I am, she would never show these emotions! Who is she? How does she know them?*

Arya said, "Then?"

Julian smiled and said, "Don't worry; my story has a nice ending. That night, I might have been a monster, but someone saved me, so I was able to become a good human being. He even gave me his surname." Arya didn't notice that he was talking about a supernatural being. She didn't imagine that he might be one of them.

After his session, Arya reminded Julian that he had once said that he wanted to be a good person and that he contributes to society for that reason. She said that she understood what he meant now, and she apologized for mocking his sincerity when he said it. She meant every word, but something made Julian freeze, and he left with shock.

As he walked away stiffly, Arya thought about the person whom Julian said saved him. Something about it bothered her, but she waved off her suspicions.

In the meantime, one of the magical servants who stalked Julian by Caleb's orders, Menar, the servant, called Caleb and reported to him about Julian.

Cornelia, who was beside Caleb in the car, told him that his association with servants was why Arkon hates him. Caleb replied that Arkon hated him for numerous reasons and started up the car, and he said that they have to see one's true feelings in order to understand them.

Meanwhile, Julian was still shaking from Arya's apology when Secretary Nigel called him about an upcoming appointment. So he headed to his meeting, unaware that Caleb and Cornelia were watching him.

When Julian arrived at the meeting spot, he left his car and walked toward the building. Cornelia and Caleb were watching him from far away. Cornelia asked, "What are you planning to do?"

Caleb replied, "We must make sure of what Arkon said."

Cornelia said, "No, I don't think that we must do this because what will we do if he is a human?"

Caleb stared at her and said, "Well, that will be his fate!" When Cornelia tried to stop him, he snapped his fingers. A nearby car started and aimed itself at Julian. Another finger snap caused the car to accelerate, and Julian saw it bearing down on him. Caleb eagerly awaited the results of his experience, but an instant before the car slammed into Julian, Cornelia threw out a hand, and the car spun away.

Julian never moved a muscle, but he finally saw Caleb watching him. Caleb gave him a smirk before he followed Cornelia to ask why she interfered—does she have feelings for Julian? Cornelia said, "It's because of you, you jerk!" She asked him what he'd do if Julian were human, reminding him that their job as the veil guards prohibits harming humans. Breaking that rule would get him banned from the great realm of Meridian.

She asked angrily why Caleb was so out of control, and he actually looked chastened for once. Cornelia called Arkon to tell him that Julian will be on the alert, so Arkon called Caleb and told him to set up a meeting with Julian!

In the meantime, Arya was in her office, busy overanalyzing Arkon's invitation to go home together, alternately swooning and telling herself that he just wanted to go for a drive. Nani burst into her office, dying of curiosity to know why she couldn't read Arkon's fate when she saw him last time in her divination booth. Arya took Nani to a nearby restaurant, and she explained everything to her about Arkon, Meridian, and everything that happened with her, but Nani couldn't believe it. She asked, "Are you sick?"

Arya sighed and replied, "If you don't believe me and you are a hex, then who shall believe me!"

Meanwhile, Arkon went to Julian's land. He opened the giant iron gate and walked inside. He walked among the trees to see Julian standing there, watching him approach. Julian walked and stood in front of him. Arkon said, "I thought that you would show yourself after I exposed you that day."

"You recognized me. That means you are the king, or you would be the next king of Meridian," Julian replied.

"If you know that, you should show your respect to your king!" Arkon said.

"I don't belong to your world. You are not a king of mine!" Julian responded.

Then Arkon said immediately, "Are you saying that you are a human?"

Julian replied, "I don't care what you and your kind think about me. I don't want to fight with you or with any one of your kind!"

"We also don't care at all, but I want to check something first. If what I think is right, that will prove you are a legendary monster!" Arkon replied.

Julian's facial expressions changed, and he said, "What are you talking about?"

Arkon lunged at Julian and ripped open his shirt, revealing a glowing mark on Julian's collarbone. Arkon said, "This is Van's mark, the mark of the earth element guard. Why does it appear on your body?" Then he screamed, "Where is Van?"

Julian took Arkon's hand off his shirt and yelled right back, "I don't know him."

"Then explain to me this mark," Arkon replied.

Julian said, "I'm not forced to explain anything to you." When Arkon tried to punch him, someone yelled 'Arkon' and pulled him away magically.

Arkon turned and found Cornelia. Then he said, "What are you doing?"

"Leave," Cornelia replied.

Arkon thundered, "What?"

"Leave! Do you want to be humiliated? You are powerless," Cornelia said. The tension was broken by a small voice calling out to Julian—it's the little blind girl. She asked Julian if someone was there; he told her no and glared at Arkon and Cornelia until they left.

Once alone, Cornelia told Arkon that he had nothing to prove to them. She apologized for losing the magical stones, asking him to wait and let her and Caleb solve the problem and find Van. "Don't interfere with Julian because you are going to get hurt," Cornelia said. Arkon stared at her and nodded, but he wasn't fully satisfied.

When it was time to head home, Arya fidgeted, thinking about Arkon. Matt poked his head in from the office door to remind her that it was her mother's memorial day, so Arya rushed home alone to cook up some ceremonial offerings. She was so unsettled that she knocked a hot skillet onto the floor. She couldn't believe how she forgot her mother's memorial. Alone, with no family, no friends, no people around, she sat on the floor and started crying. Meanwhile, Arkon heard the crash as he had arrived home, and he went inside to find Arya curled into a ball, crying her heart out. Gently, he asked, "What happened?" Arya sobbed that nothing was going right because of him!

He accompanied her to her mother's grave, where she joked darkly for him to be careful because sometimes her mother tried to come out. Arkon rolled his eyes. Then he waited while she prayed and greeted her mother. She apologized for coming empty-handed, blaming it on being possessed by a weird immortal.

They sat on the grass together. Arya started talking. "My father abandoned my mother and me; my mother was angry all the time, and she was always drunk. Then she died of liver cancer. I hated my father very much, but I also hated my mother. I think that both of my parents were very selfish, and they cared only about themselves." She looked at Arkon and asked him, "Throughout the 4000 years you lived, did you do something that embarrassed you, or did you regret something?"

Arkon's answer was clear and confident. "No."

Arya said, "Well, I regret many things, and I felt embarrassed once. I felt very embarrassed that day, and I don't think that I will feel like that again. After my mother passed away, I directed my aversion toward my father, and my life was a mess. Someday I wanted to take revenge on him, so I jumped in the river in the middle of winter; it was freezing, and all that I wanted was to die. However, when I did it, I wanted to get out of there. I felt that I would freeze. I learned swimming in my childhood, which kept me alive then, but I couldn't swim again after that accident. That is really embarrassing when I think about it now." Her cheeks became red because Arkon was watching her closely.

"I'm glad that the dark covered the place," Arya said.

Arkon replied, "Be thankful because I lost my powers because if I had them now, this place would be gleaming!"

"What would you do if you still had it?" Arya asked.

He made a gesture in the air that usually summons bright water fireflies, then Arya teased him when nothing happened. He tried again, telling Arya to look with her heart. This time, a tiny blue light appeared, then several more. The twinkly water fireflies enchanted Arya, and Arkon watched her as she smiled.

Later, when they arrived back home, Arya asked what Arkon meant when he asked her to go home together. He said he meant he'd pick her up, but then she was gone when he got earlier to her clinic. He waved her inside imperiously. Then she listened as he went to the roof. Arya knocked on the interior door to his room and asked if he wanted to go home together tomorrow since they couldn't make it today. She repeated her promise to take him to nice places and feed him good food, and Arkon smiled the tiniest little smile as he agreed.

The next morning, she woke up excited and brought up the land sale contract to Tynar, asking if selling it would interfere with Arkon becoming king. He said it probably won't, and she told him that Arkon said that there are those in his world who are always on alert for an opportunity. And Tynar nodded.

When Arya went to her job at the clinic, Matt complained that they'd had no patients at all today. But instead of her usual pessimistic acceptance, Arya told him to pass out business cards and update their blog! She instructed him to make another loan request of Salar's father, the patient who tried to drown himself and was saved by Arkon—his father was a banker.

Then Arya took her contract and went to meet Julian. When she arrived at his office, she told him that she had changed her mind about selling the land. Julian asked, "Why have you changed your mind? Is there something bad that happened?"

Arya replied, "I can't apologize enough, Mr. Julian, but I really can't explain this."

"Okay, I understand. I will hold a meeting to discuss it," Julian replied. Then Arya left, and she was sad because she did that. Arkon called her to confirm their meeting, so Arya went on her way, waiting for him to come. She crashed into an old lady with white hair. Arya bowed down and picked up the woman's stuff that had dropped on the ground. The woman took Arya's hand and said, "Thank you, kind girl!" Then she looked at Arya's necklace and touched it with her hand, and Arya noticed the ring—the same ring with the tree sign on it! The woman said, "This is a unique necklace. Protect it!" Arya noticed Arkon on the other side; when she turned to the woman, she was gone. Arya turned left and right, but she had vanished.

When Arkon saw Arya on the other side, his eyes lit up when he spotted something shining. But then he seemed to see something that alarmed him, and he broke into a run.

As Arya was watching, Arkon raced across the street towards her, a look of fury on his face. He approached her, and he looked astonished. He pointed at her hand; she looked down and saw something shining. Arkon spoke.

"The…the magical map!"

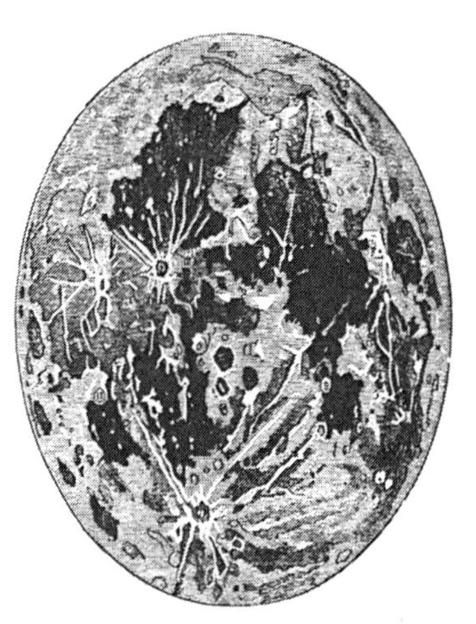

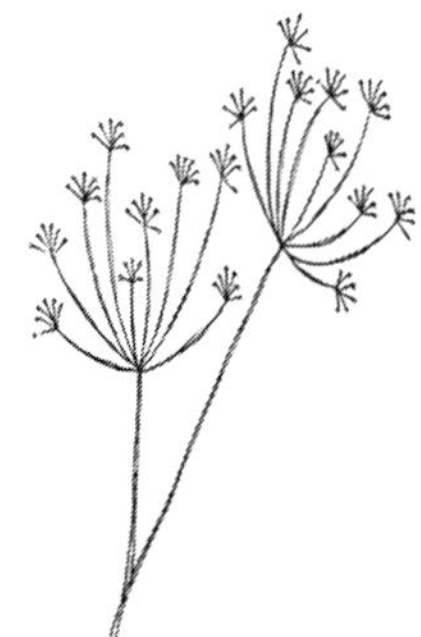

In the meantime, in Meridian, Queen Wera was watching what was happening with Arkon and Arya on Visions Lake. She smiled and said, "My son, you are late this time. I thought you would have found out earlier!"

On earth, Julian was on the balcony of his office, thinking about Arya. What she said about the land contract, he thought that the reason behind canceling the sale was Arkon. His phone rang; he picked it up, and it was Caleb's voice. "It seems that you live a welfare life, half-immortal and half-human. I see that you planted a tree here with various roses. It seems that you pretend that you are a good human," Caleb said.

"What do you want?" Julian asked.

"I want to know you better, and that sign on your body does not fit you, so let's talk about that too," Caleb replied. A small voice piped up, and Julian looked stricken when Caleb handed the phone to the little blind girl. Julian bellowed that the little girl has nothing to do with this. Caleb told him to come quickly, and he ended the call and sent the girl away with Menar, the silent magical servant.

When Julian arrived, Caleb officially introduced himself and Cornelia. Caleb noted that Julian didn't act like an immortal because he was so nice to the blind girl. He said that when they were younger, Cornelia thought of Julian as a disgrace to the world of Meridian, but now she was giving him a chance.

Caleb added that Arkon's feelings are clear, and as for himself, "I just hate you. I always will." Cornelia told Julian to explain why he carried the earth guard's mark (Van's mark). Julian said that he met the owner of the mark when he first arrived in this world! Someone had flown at me out of nowhere, and we'd gone crashing to the ground. Julian said that a bolt of lightning hit the person in the back, and that's when he got the mark.

Caleb said, "Did you kill him? I heard that what you do is kill, and you already killed many immortals back in Meridian."

Julian lost his control and yelled, "That is not true—"

Caleb interrupted him and said, "Did you wanted to feel like immortals? But you are a half one!"

Cornelia screamed, "Caleb, stop!" Julian told them that the person who fell on him didn't move after being hit by lightning, so Julian just left. Cornelia was furious, but Julian argued that he wasn't yet the person he is now, explaining that he was frightened, so he ran. But Caleb said that lightning doesn't harm immortals, convinced that Julian must have done something to Van.

In the meantime, Arkon couldn't believe what he saw. He asked Arya, "What is this? Where did you get this?" Arya was also in shock because she didn't notice how she got the shining map.

She only uttered, "It must be the woman!"

"Which woman?" Arkon asked.

"I don't know; there was a woman here, but she's gone!" Arya replied. Then she asked, "Is this the map that you were looking for? Is this the map that Tynar lost on his way to our world?"

Arkon sighed and replied, "Yes. It's the magical map."

While the three, Cornelia, Caleb, and Cornelia, were arguing, Cornelia got a phone call from Arkon, and he told her that he had found the map, so Cornelia was in shock. She instructed Caleb that they have no business here.

Arya and Arkon were in the car. Arkon was holding the map and said, "The map is pointing to the veil guards, and now it shows Van's place, and it's not far. I can't believe that he is in this world, and they failed to find him."

Eventually, Arya asked if this meant Arkon was leaving, and he sent her a look and quietly said, "Yes." Then Arya forced herself to smile and congratulated him.

Arkon and Arya ended up at night in a random park holding flashlights, searching for Van, the third guard. As they were walking, suddenly Arkon said, "Don't expect a lot of things from that man."

"Which man?" Arya asked.

Arkon replied, "Julian."

"Why do you always say that? It seems that he can help me more than you!" Arya replied.

"You are saying that because of what he looks like," Arkon said.

Arya replied, "Don't worry, I'm a psychiatrist. I know how to know the deep inside of human beings."

She said that Julian was an almost perfect human being. She admonished Arkon not to be prejudiced, so Arkon asked how much she knew about Julian. He snapped that she seemed easy to fool, and he started to walk again. She tried to follow him. Arya tripped and grabbed the back of Arkon's jacket. He looked at her and said, "Hold my hand."

She replied, "No, thanks, I can walk alone! I can go wherever I want."

When they got to the spot the coordinates indicated, they found themselves in front of a man who was industriously digging holes in the ground. Arkon recognized him immediately. "Van, what are you doing here?"

The silver-haired man turned and saw Arkon and Arya. Arya opened her mouth in a state of shock. She asked, "Is that your friend Van?" The tall man with a godly white face and blue eyes made Arya forget all words. Van's clothes were filthy.

The man stated, "Do I know you?"

Arkon was shocked and uttered, "What? What do you mean?" Van approached them, and Arya hid behind Arkon's back. Arkon realized that Van had lost his memories because he was the closest to him back in Meridian.

Arkon said, "Sorry, my friend, and hit him on his head with the flashlight!"

"Oh my god, what did you do?" Arya croaked.

Arkon lifted him and said, "Come on; we will go to Caleb's place."

In Caleb's penthouse, all of them were standing above Van's head. They deduced that Van had lost both his memory and his powers when he lost his earth mark to Julian. Caleb used his powers on his head and said, "He will take a long time sleeping because he needs to recover."

Cornelia demanded that Arya leave since there was no place for the immortal's servant! Arya jumped up and said she'd go home alone, assuming that Arkon wouldn't be back tonight. When Caleb offered her a ride, he earned a death glare from Cornelia. Before leaving, Arya requested Cornelia not speak to her in banal. Cornelia informed Arya that she was a mighty immortal and the most powerful guard for the veil, but Arya cut off Cornelia with a bored, "Yes, yes…" Then she left.

Arya went down to her car and got in it. She was feeling strange; she couldn't admit that to herself, but she couldn't bear that Arkon would leave soon.

Up in Caleb's penthouse, Cornelia tattled to Arkon, saying that Caleb accused Julian of killing Van. She fussed at Caleb and Arkon for ignoring her advice to leave Julian alone. Caleb asked why they had to fear him, so Cornelia told him to grow up. Arkon backed her up and told Caleb not to provoke Julian anymore. Caleb seethed, and Cornelia told Arkon to go back to the realm of Meridian once he got the stones from Van and find the Great Jewel of Meridian.

Arkon went to the roof of the high building that overlooked the city lights. Cornelia followed him and said from behind, "You don't like high places."

She approached and stood beside him. "Isn't that gorgeous? During the night and day, humans have a lot of things that we don't have in our world. Sometimes I think in humans' lives, it's true that they have a lot of difficulties, but they also don't consider the good things and the grace they have."

"Caleb loves the life here. What about you?" Arkon asked.

"Except the nice clothes here, I love nothing, and I always think about going back to Meridian, but I can't. Protecting the veil is my mission, and I don't know when we can stop doing that and live our lives," Cornelia replied.

"We don't know. Maybe this day will come soon!" Arkon replied.

Cornelia's facial expressions changed, then she asked, "What do you mean by that?"

Arkon stared at her and sighed; he spoke no word. She asked, "We found Van. Why do you look sad?"

"No, I'm happy," Arkon replied.

"Yesterday—"

Arkon interrupted her: "I told you, I want to go back fast."

Cornelia said, "The girl, Arya, our servant—"

Arkon interrupted her again, "Before I came here, Lady Halinor told me that this time would be different from the past times, and she talked about a legend, an ancient legend, and asked me to find the reason why the jewel was sent to earth with every king's inauguration, and now I'm about to leave; I don't know what she meant."

"Don't wonder; she lived for thousands of years. I think she is crazy. No one saw her in 1400 years, so don't listen to her."

Arkon stared at her as he said nothing, then said, "Really?"

She asserted, "Yes, and I know the answer to that because I lived here long enough to know the reason behind sending the jewel here with every inauguration. It's obvious because the new king must learn about humans before he takes the throne and to know why this world must stay isolated from the other worlds." The silence took hold, then Cornelia added, "But you, you learned that earlier than all of us; you know the nature of humans. Thousands of years ago, when they buried a live woman in the sea, you took her to Meridian, and you looked after her; you loved her! But she betrayed you; she betrayed the great world of Meridian. She exchanged our love for betrayal and caused chaos for the first time in Meridian. Humans are the same: cruel, greedy, and liars. What do you want to know more about them? Go back; go to your throne. Arya will no longer be your responsibility after you leave. Even if she were lucky to be your responsibility, she would remain nothing, like a piece of dust. I don't know why you look hesitant, but you should know that I will not just be watching this time."

In the meantime, Arya visited her friend Nani, who fussed at her for choosing the wrong profession because she's too sensitive. Arya whined that she only has two friends, and both of them are nags. Nani said that Matt was only trying to repay her father for taking him in by taking care of Arya. But Arya said that when she sees Matt, it reminds her that her father abandoned her to take care of other children. When Nani asked if Arya would be happier if Matt were gone, Arya froze as the thought horrified her. Not wanting to go home yet, Arya invited Nani to hang out, but Nani declined.

When Arya left Nani's booth, she stopped in a park and got on a swing. She called Matt and asked him if he wanted to hang out, but he replied that he had plans. So she headed home alone, and even though she knew better, she was still hoping that Arkon would be waiting under the streetlight as usual. When she arrived, he wasn't there, so she sighed heavily, telling herself that she always walked alone before. She stopped to look at the spot where Arkon drew their names on the brick wall; then her phone rang.

"Hello…" It was Arkon, and Arya answered just as she got inside her gate. She stopped when she saw Arkon there, waiting for her! The silence took hold, and she remained still, staring into his eyes while holding the phone. She felt like her heart wanted to get out of her chest. She spoke with glamour shining in her eyes. "You said you would not come today! Is his memory back?"

Arkon replied, "No, not yet. They said it would take a few days."

"So why are you here?" Arya asked.

"I came to turn the lights on!" He put the phone down, walked to the light button, and turned it on. She approached him, her heart pounding. Arya plucked at Arkon's jacket, and he turned to see her crying. He asked, "Why are you crying?"

She just replied, "I'm smiling."

Giving in to an impulse, she wrapped her arms around Arkon in a back hug. He turned in her arms, then took a step closer, leaning in as if to kiss her.

But Arya stepped back and said, "I'm sorry." Arkon dropped her hand to let her go inside. She opened the door, stared at him, and said, "Good night."

The following day, Julian was sitting in the garden outside his office, looking pained at the memory of Caleb saying that he could kill with just a touch. He crouched next to the flowerbed and reached out, and the patch of flowers withered on the spot. On a nearby balcony, Miranda happened to see, and the sight struck her with confused fear.

She thought about it; then she went to Julian's office. She confronted him, "I saw everything; I saw what you did to the flowers!"

"What are you talking about?" Julian asked.

And he tensed as she got at what he was doing, but then she guessed that it was a magic trick, and then he sighed heavily.

But his face hardened as she went on about how he shouldn't do such creepy magic, and when she turned away nervously, he grabbed her in a back hug. It was far from romantic—black smoke seeped from his hands as he struggled to keep control. After a few seconds, the smoke receded back into his hands, and he let Miranda go. He apologized and told her to leave.

Julian couldn't believe that he did that and put Miranda's life in danger because he couldn't control his powers.

Miranda walked away in a daze, not even noticing Secretary Nigel on the stairs. He looked concerned and asked if she was sick, but she just stared at him, then kept walking. She was shocked because she didn't know about that behavior; she started thinking that maybe he liked her.

After Miranda left the office, Herbert, the magical servant, entered immediately! He said, "She left in a hurry, so I felt curious. Did she see something?"

"I felt nervous," Julian said.

"Okay, then let's continue our conversation that we held earlier!" Herbert replied. He sat, then he asked, "When did you come here?"

Julian replied, "Ten years ago."

"Did you escape from the cave? How could you escape from Meridian?"

"They kicked me out of Meridian."

"After he took you from your mother, why did he leave you?" Herbert asked.

"I didn't know that you were in this world; you didn't come to the cave for a long time, so I thought that you didn't want to come again," Julian replied.

"I came here 500 years ago. I got a lot of trouble in Meridian, so I escaped, and I couldn't go back there. When Prince Arkon brought the bloody rock from the land, I knew that you were here, so I searched for you," Herbert stated.

Praising Julian for his control over his powers, Herbert reminded him that he once said that thorns needed to be removed for flowers to grow. But he admitted that he regretted it because, after three thousand years locked in that cave, he felt like what he said stole Julian's hope.

He told Julian that he wouldn't see him again now that he confirmed that it was really him. Julian stopped him to ask about Arya and why she seemed to know who Arkon and the other immortals were.

In the meantime, Arya invited Arkon to have breakfast with her, and he eyed the mess on his plate and the worse mess in the kitchen, quipping that the rice omelet didn't look like something that required two hours' preparation. He tried it. Then he declared it absolutely…tasteless!

Arya whined that it wouldn't kill him to lie to save her feelings, but he said that he only tells the truth. Arya scoffed, recalling his lie about the reason the immortals punished her family, accusing him of being afraid to face the truth. Laughing wryly, Arya said that the immortals must have been very afraid of her family. Arkon just asked her if they should go home together, but it was her day off, so she suggested they do something else!

They deep-cleaned the entire house, and to his credit, Arkon applied himself enthusiastically. He was still grumpy with Arya because she forced him into this, and some of his techniques were hilarious. He changed a light bulb by holding it with both hands and spinning in circles.

Arkon saw Arya teetering on a stool, trying to reach some books. He stepped onto the stool behind her and got the books down, leaning in just a bit closer than necessary, flustering her. After they cleaned every shelf, Arya said, "Oh my God, I haven't cleaned the house for a decade!"

"Why?" Arkon asked.

"This house used to be clean in the past. Everyone who lived here used to clean because there were a lot of people living here," Arya replied.

Arya flopped onto the floor, inviting Arkon to join her and stretch his back. He refused, grumpy again, snapping, "I'm still a man," when she challenged him. Arya huffed, so Arkon lay down right next to her. She pushed him, and he said blandly, "You told me to lie down."

Arya tried to scoot away, but Arkon scooted closer, repeating, "You told me to lie down."

Arkon rolled towards Arya until she was trapped against the table, and their faces were inches apart. Arkon whispered in a sexy voice, "You told me to lie down." Arya stammered that she didn't mean this, and Arkon slammed a hand on the table, trapping her in his arms. Then he said, "How dare you try to seduce me!" Arya denied it, but Arkon said that newspapers and TV had taught him that all men are not trusted in this world. He ordered Arya not to tell men to lie down next to her or hug them from behind and cry, as she did to him yesterday. He leaned very close, and Arya closed her eyes and braced herself for a kiss. But Arkon just got up and left her there.

At night, after their hard work, they got out to walk and talk. In the meantime, Herbert was stalking after them; he realized that Arya was an immortal's servant. He went to tell Julian immediately. Julian asked him, "When did she become a servant for them?"

"Her ancestors committed a grave sin thousands of years ago," Herbert replied.

Herbert added that it was Julian who needed an immortals' servant most because she would understand and accept him as he is, and that the cycle of being born, growing up, then dying over and over for eternity was too vicious for Julian to handle alone.

Meanwhile, Arya and Arkon got back to her house. Arkon followed Arya into her home, as he belonged there, heading for the door connecting to his room. Arya insisted he use the outside door. He stared at her. Then he pouted as he left. Arya was very confused with her emotions because she wanted him to stay, and her mind told her to let him go because he didn't belong there.

In the meantime, in Julian's resort, Cornelia went back to the movie set, where they tried to film the kissing scene again, but her co-star passed out again. She threatened them to quit this miserable cast, and Caleb told her to just make movies that weren't romantic. Cornelia and Caleb were walking in the corner. When Julian approached them, Caleb told him that they had found Van thanks to him. He seemed like he was trying to be nice, but then he sneered that Julian ruined things and the immortals' guards fixed him, which was the crucial difference between them. Cornelia's facial expressions changed because of Caleb's behavior. She walked and left him. He turned to Julian and said, "See you later!" Then he followed Cornelia.

Caleb caught up to Cornelia, who asked angrily if he had a personal problem with Julian. "Your anger is not conditional, and I think you have something personal you don't want to share. That's why you are feeling angry at Julian, right?" Caleb asked why she didn't practice her kissing scene ahead of time in an odd change of subject. Caleb got a call from Menar, who was one of the magical servants, and he asked Cornelia to leave, said that he would leave immediately to take care of something, and reminded Cornelia to take care of Van.

Julian came back to his office feeling sad about what Caleb had said. With the final plans looming, his secretary Nigel reminded him to settle the land sale with Arya soon. Julian suddenly realized something, and he flipped through a portfolio to find photos of Arya's land. And he was shocked to see the land of the gate, and only now did he realize where he had entered this world from and why Arya had asked to cancel the contract. So he visited the land, remembering the night he tumbled into the human realm. Looking around, Julian compared the landscape with his memory of this land and found it to be a match. He climbed to the top of the gate and laughed like a crazy man. Caleb's voice called out, asking what Julian planned to do. He punched Julian, accusing him of approaching Arya for the land. But Julian reminded Caleb that he said Julian ruins things, and he said what he plans to do with the land!

Before he left, he told Caleb that he did make Van the way he is. He screamed that the immortals think of themselves as saviors, and he asked if they planned to kill him. With bare teeth, he asked, "But can you do that? Can you kill me? Are you strong enough to do that?"

When Caleb heard that, he disappeared instantly and appeared next to Arkon. Arkon asked, "What are you doing here?"

Caleb reported to Arkon that Arya had already sold the land to Julian. Arkon was confident that the portal gate wouldn't change just because the owner changed, but Caleb said that Julian could make the gate unusable in other ways, such as by filling the land with people. He reminded Arkon that if the immortals can't visit the human realm and the main gate is closed, then the veil will fade and the realm of humans will be permanently isolated.

Caleb scoffed that, as irresponsible as he can be, he's never forgotten his identity because he fell for a human. He said contemptuously that it was not even Arkon's first time. Then he added that what annoyed him most was that Arkon played the victim and made him feel guilty.

Just as Arkon stood to hit Caleb, Caleb's phone rang. He answered it, then he told Arkon, "Go see what your servant—no, your *woman*—is up to."

Meanwhile, Arya met Julian at a restaurant, where he asked for the real reason that she didn't want to sell her land and whether it was because of the person she once said opposed the sale.

"Yes, actually; it's the real reason, but he didn't order me to do that. The decision is totally mine. I feel like I want to do that to be better," Arya said.

"Well, not everybody rejects 100 thousand dollars to feel better!" Julian replied.

"I have been taught that the person who has more should help those who have less. My father taught that," Arya replied.

Julian asked, "Is that person the same person whom I met in my hotel?" Arya stared at him, but she spoke no word. Then Julian said, "That man doesn't seem like he has less!"

"Losing the money will do less harm to me than losing the land for that man," Arya replied.

Julian said, "I know that you always care about others. I know now your point of view, and I will tell the others in the company. Also, I want you to know that helping others and the strong people must help the weak people it's the rule of my life, but I disagree with you that the man you meant is weaker than you! I will call you soon to tell you the result." He stood and left the place.

Outside the restaurant, Julian saw that Arkon was watching them through the window. Julian told him that he was the only person whose emotions he couldn't read, but it was obvious that Arkon was feeling anger, contempt, and confusion.

Julian approached Arkon until he became two steps away from him. Then Arkon said, "Nothing would change even if you had the portal gate."

"That is not important to me at all! I don't care about the gate or the land. What is only important to me now is Arya! She will be my first and strongest desire since I came into this world, and I will win her heart very easily," Julian replied.

Arkon's anger controlled him; he growled that she was the immortals' servant, but Julian retorted that this was the human world. "It's my turf," Julian declared. He smiled and continued, "Oh, one last thing, Arya called you a passing wind, which has stopped blowing, and that gave me the necessary power to fight, and I want you to tell Caleb that I have no interest in the immortals or their realm, so they should go home and leave this world to me." Then he turned and left before Arya got out of the restaurant.

As Arya left the restaurant and headed off, not seeing Arkon, she called him, and he almost didn't answer, and when he did, he just answered yes or no to her questions.

She invited him to go to eat since he was out, so she waited for him at their tree. Arkon still looked thunderous as he approached her, and he just glared furiously at her when she greeted him. Finally, he asked if she sold her land to Julian, and Arya nodded that she did.

Arkon rescinded what he said about selling being her choice. But Arya said that she was already canceling the sale, growing angry herself as she admitted that she felt guilty for selling what was hers.

"Your request to sell the land is not important, and what you did with him is not important to me either!" Arkon said.

"Not important! Then why did I feel miserable all this time, and why did I spend time and money on something that is not even important to you?" Arya replied.

Arkon replied, "You were right; I will leave soon, and you belong to this world, so we shouldn't spend time making each other happy." His heart was hurting when he spoke these words. He turned and walked to leave.

Arya said softly, "In times of hardship, those who smile are first-rate. Those who endure are second-rate. And those who cry are third-rate." Arkon turned to see Arya crying, and she added, "You made me third-rate." She sobbed, "I tried to harden my heart, trying my best to keep tears at bay so I could survive. I thought I was first-rate after meeting you, but now I see that I'm not."

Arkon let out a sigh, as if letting go of a burden. He walked back to Arya, looking at her sadly as he said, "I'm going to leave. I have to leave." He reached out to grasp her hand, pulled her in, and kissed her.

Arya stood frozen, and Arkon pulled back just enough to look her in the eyes. He repeated, "I said I'm going to leave." Then he pulled her close again.

Arya closed her eyes, and this time, when Arkon kissed her, she kissed him back. The moment felt like a long day. Suddenly, a phone rang and interrupted them; it was Cornelia. "Van woke up!" Arkon opened his eyes widely, as he didn't expect that at this moment.

Arya asked, "Did he wake up?"

"Yes, he did," Arkon replied. Arya drove him to Caleb's penthouse. They were both silent. Arkon realized that once Van had woken up, he only had a few days in this world because he had the stones and would soon find the jewel. He couldn't feel happy that his mission would be accomplished soon because that meant he would leave Arya. When they arrived, Arya said, "You must go now!" She smiled a pale smile; then Arkon stared at her.

She added, "Show me the stones when you take them. I have a curiosity to see them." He nodded and left the car.

Arkon watched her drive away. Then a voice called his name. He saw Van standing close by, holding out his arms for a hug. Arkon returned his hug enthusiastically. Van was his close friend back in Meridian before he became one of the guards to protect the veil.

Up in Caleb's penthouse, the five—Arkon, Cornelia, Van, Caleb, and Tynar—sat to talk. Van told them that when he lost his memory, he woke up in a hospital with no clue who he was or what had happened. The person who brought him to the hospital couldn't be reached, so he ended up wandering, homeless, and working small jobs until he ended up at a temple. "When they saw my face in the temple, they thought I was one of the gods, but on that day when Arkon found me, something made me leave the temple and guided to that park," Van said.

Arkon said, "I know that you lost consciousness that day because lightning hit you, but I don't understand why you lost your memory for eight years!"

"We know why! Because of Julian. He confessed that to Caleb earlier today," Cornelia said.

Arkon stared angrily, then he asked Van, "Did you find the stones? Where are they?"

Van held out a hand. A bright light shone in his palm when he opened it, which materialized into three stones that floated in the air, marked with a glowing circle. Tynar sighed, and Cornelia was pleased because she wanted him to go back and leave Arya.

Cornelia said, "What are you waiting for? Use it; find the Great Jewel of Meridian."

Arkon raised his hands and said, "In the name of Meridian, I order you to find the Great Jewel of Meridian." The three stones spun in the air in a circle, then created a great circle, transforming into a gate. On the other side, it showed Arya's house! Cornelia stood and looked at the others and said, "What? How is that possible? The jewel is in the servant's house!"

When they wanted to cross the gate, the gate immediately closed itself. Caleb asked, "What is going on?"

Arkon said, "Let's go." He took the stones and ordered Cornelia to drive.

On their way to Arya's house, Van said, "Can I stay with you there? Because Cornelia and her husband's home make me feel claustrophobic!"

Cornelia was so flustered at his calling Caleb her husband. She pulled over to yell at Van. Van asked if he remembered wrong since he clearly recalled Caleb telling him that he and Cornelia were engaged. Van added that Caleb said they hadn't spent a night together yet and that he couldn't wait, and Cornelia let out a bloodcurdling scream to shut him up.

Speaking of Caleb, Cornelia told them that Caleb had been acting strange lately, being overly sensitive and hostile to Julian. Van defended Julian, saying that he was using his powers and making Van lose his memory was unintentional, but Cornelia objected, saying that Caleb thinks it was intentional. Tynar wondered if they should consider Julian a human or an immortal since they couldn't harm him if he were a human.

When they arrived at Arya's home, Arkon ordered the others to go up to the rooftop, and he went to knock on Arya's door. She heard the knocking, and she was about to go to sleep. She went downstairs and opened the door. Arkon said, "Sorry, but I want to show you something."

He got in and sat on the couch. Arya approached him and sat next to him. She asked, "Is everything okay? Did you find the stones and the jewel?"

He put his hand out and opened it, and the three magical stones appeared. Arya was surprised to see them. "Oh my God. It's stunning. I didn't see anything like that in my whole life, but wait, that means you found the jewel, right?"

Arkon replied, "No, when I ordered the stones to show me the place of the jewel, they created a gate and showed your house! And that's what led us here; that's mean the jewel is here! In your home."

Arya laughed, and she was shocked. "What are you talking about? The object that you were looking for all this time is here! In my home?"

"I don't understand either, but the magical objects can't be mistaken," Arkon replied. Then he put the stones on the table, waved with his hands, and ordered, "In the name of Meridian, show me the place of the jewel."

The stones floated in the air and started to shine a great light. Then Arya panicked and stood away. The stones approached Arya, made a circle around her, and floated in circles around her over and over! Arya screamed, and Arkon stood amused. He ordered the stones to stop.

When the stones fell on the ground, Arya was freaked out, so Arkon approached and hugged her. "What is going on?" Arya wondered.

"I don't know. I didn't see something like that before I asked for the jewel. I am actually confused. I'm sorry for what just happened," Arkon replied.

He took her up to her bed; he went to the roof to tell the others. When he told them, Cornelia said, "That couldn't be happening. The stones can't make a mistake. There is something wrong with this girl." Arkon immediately ordered Cornelia to leave. She stared at him angrily and walked. Then she turned to him and said, "You must go back to Meridian and tell the king and the queen about that." Then she left.

Van said, "Maybe she is right. You should go and ask because this is the first time to use the stones."

"You and Cornelia are convinced that the problem is something in the stones, but I say the opposite!" Arkon replied.

"What do you mean?" Van asked. But Arkon spoke no word. Then Van continued, "The immortals' servants. When Caleb talked to Queen Wera into creating them as a punishment, many immortals had opposed, and one of them was Cornelia. She thought it was unfair to make humans take responsibility for what the immortals did."

"Why are you bringing this up?" Arkon asked.

"I'm your friend. I'm your friend, Your Highness. We spent thousands of years together back in Meridian. I know you very well if you allow me to say that you love her! You love this human girl, but you are afraid to repeat the experience again after all these years, and also I'm sure that deep inside, you are happy because you didn't find the jewel and that it gave you more time here! But I want to tell you something fundamental, and I think the others don't know that the Great Jewel of Meridian can't show itself until the desire of finding it will be a real pure desire," Van replied.

Arkon sighed and said, "When I arrived on earth, I saw the gate guard lady, Halinor; she told me a lot of things, legends and these sorts of things. I remember what she said, but I can't understand why she said that."

"Now that you mention Halinor, I remember something vital about that day when I lost my memory," Van replied.

Arkon asked him, "What is that thing?"

"Nothing; it's not important. Go to sleep now," Van replied.

The next morning, Arya woke up in a daze. She did not remember last night. Very clearly, she looked at her necklace and thought, *Oh, I forgot to take off the necklace yesterday.* Arkon went downstairs and approached Arya's door again. This time, before he knocked, she opened the door. The air was awkward and uncomfortable between them, and Arya left for work with hardly a word to Arkon. "Are you leaving?" Arkon asked.

"Yes, I'm busy. Goodbye," Arya replied.

At her clinic, Matt was startled to find Arya at the office, mopping the ground before him, and she told him that they were working extended hours from now on. He fussed over her and took over the mopping; she went to her office, but she hardly concentrated, remembering Arkon's kiss and how he said he was leaving over and over in her mind. Suddenly, her phone rang. Julian called her and asked her to meet him this afternoon.

In the meantime, at a coffee shop, Caleb told his silent minion, Menar, that Julian said they couldn't do anything to him. "We must take revenge on him for what he did!"

In Julian's office, Arya arrived for her meeting with Julian, where he told her that the land sale contract was canceled but that there was a high cancellation fee. He offered to let her pay half of it by providing psychological services to his hotel employees, who often need to unburden the stresses of customer service. As for the rest, Julian split the cost between her working on his farm, taking her up on her offer to help out and in treatment sessions for his insomnia. "And you will pay nothing for the contract cancellation fees," Julian said.

When Arya came back to her clinic, she found Nani waiting for her. They entered her office, and Nani said she was there because Arya showed up in her dreams. She came to see if Arya had good news, but she could see that something was wrong. Arya said she was trying to solve a complex math problem whose answer she already knew, but the solving process and the answer didn't match!

As Arya walked home that night, she decided just to blame the math and find a creative solution. She paused before rounding the corner again, bracing herself in anticipation of seeing the streetlight empty. But that night, Arkon was there, waiting for her, so she approached him and asked, "Why?" He said he was giving up on trying to regain his powers, his usual excuse for being there.

He said her name, "Arya—" But she interrupted to tell him that she had been solving a math problem all day.

She said that she thought of a solution to stop things now rather than start something new. She said that she wanted to end on a beautiful note, and she asked for Arkon's help. Arkon asked, "What do you want me to do?"

So Arya told him, "Treat me as you did before yesterday." He didn't look happy, but he walked her home without argument.

Arkon woke up early the following day, and he was surprised to see Arya go to work early. When she told him vaguely that she had changed her office hours in order to sort out someone's mess, he admitted that he wanted to challenge her about it. But he promised to behave as long as he was here and asked what Arya needed from him. She said, "Money," in that drawn-out way that had become their private joke. Arkon blinked and twitched, then he told her to forget what he just said. Chuckling, Arya said, "You should throw a farewell party before you go." But he said he had no money. Arya told him, "Go and earn some, then!" She opened the iron gate and got out. Her fake smile vanished, and she was agitated, but she couldn't show that. Meanwhile, Van was watching them from the roof. Then he revived a dead plant with a wave of his hand. When Arkon came back upstairs, Van asked if it was because of Arya that Cornelia was anxious. He said he understands Cornelia because when Arkon was going through that time, he was as sad then as he is now. "Do you know what the main difference is between humans and us?" Van asked. Then he added, "Humans living a concise life can ignore all the judgments, especially if they did something for love, but we can't do this, especially you, because you are the future of the great world of Meridian."

Arkon just stared at him and spoke no word. Van said, "But this girl is the exception to all human rules!"

Arkon was surprised and asked, "Why?"

"You must find the answer, but before that, you should make sure that what you feel is either pity toward a human girl or love. And you should know that I support you always," Van replied.

"Thank you, my friend, thank you," Arkon replied.

Meanwhile, as Julian walked through an empty parking garage, he sensed something weird. Then the lights went out, one by one. Then something slammed into Julian's knee and knocked him to the floor. Julian was struck by something that sent him spinning through the air. He was pummeled by an invisible force until he was battered and bloody, while elsewhere, Caleb was pounding the punching bag in a simultaneous rhythm. Julian was helpless to fight back because there was nothing to fight back against!

Suddenly, a pair of magical servants told each other that Caleb shouldn't make them do that. The way they talked made it sound like Caleb had put them up to this. They collapsed in cowardly fear when Julian got up, covered in blood, and locked his gaze on them. The two magical servants clutched each other, confused because they thought Julian was a human but terrified because he could still walk. Black smoke began to emanate from Julian's body as he advanced on the servants, and he raised a smoldering arm to strike them.

Someone grabbed Julian at the last second and threw him to the ground. He nearly unleashed his attack before he realized it was Herbert, and the magical servants wisely made their escape. Julian was still shaking with anger. Julian asked why they did this to him while his injuries disappeared like they never existed.

He got his answer when his phone rang. Caleb called to say that he sent the servants to prove that even the least of the immortals was stronger than Julian. He said, "I'll consider this revenge for what you did to my friend!"

"Which friend? What are you saying?" Julian asked.

"If you ever try to threaten me again, I will end you," Caleb replied. Then he ended the call. He looked at Menar, who was standing next to him, and said, "Don't stare at me in that way, even if you don't want to take revenge, but that doesn't mean I should forgive him!"

Meanwhile, Cornelia entered the training spot and said, "What are you doing here? I told you that we have to eat lunch today with Arkon and Van."

Caleb replied, "You should try boxing. It really makes the nerves relax."

Menar left them alone, and Cornelia stared at him weirdly and said, "I don't remember why he is not talking at all."

"You really don't remember? You froze his tongue when he was in Meridian!" Caleb said.

"Stop joking. I didn't do that. I would remember if I did! But I remember that he has a twin, right? Actually, I haven't seen his brother in hundreds of years," Cornelia replied.

Caleb's facial expressions changed, and he said, in order to change the subject, "Let's go."

The four immortals met for lunch. Van asked Arkon, "What's it like to feel hungry? I actually don't know how this happened to you or why you lost your powers when you came here."

"Halinor told me that every prince's experience is different from the others," Arkon replied.

Cornelia said, "That's why Arkon needs to go back to the realm of the immortals." But Caleb noted that Arkon didn't seem to want to go back.

Caleb said that he heard Julian had angered his board members by returning Arya's land. Arkon asked darkly how Caleb always knew everything. Caleb smirked, saying that he has nothing else to do. Caleb wondered what Arya had to do to get the land back, and that made Arkon angry. Cornelia asked Arkon when he would go back to Meridian, which made Caleb complain, "You are like a broken record that always repeats the same thing. What's wrong with you? Arkon will go back when he's ready because he knows what will happen if he doesn't!" Arkon stood to leave. He told Van that he'd see him when Van returned in a few days from an errand.

Van said, "Don't go before I come back; wait for me. I want to check something and come back soon." Then Arkon left, and he was thinking about what Caleb said about Arya.

Van left; then Cornelia took Caleb's hand and disappeared from the restaurant, and they moved instantly and appeared at Caleb's penthouse. Once they were alone, Cornelia blew up at Caleb for the way he was behaving toward Arkon. She accused him of being rude, irresponsible, and stubborn and said that Arkon only lets it slide because it was between him and Caleb. Caleb asked if she was angry because he provoked Arkon or because Arkon might use Caleb's words as an excuse to stay in the human realm as long as possible.

He lashed out, telling her to admit that she was insecure because of Arya. He yelled that he knew Cornelia didn't want to lose Arkon again, and he told her just to ask him for help like she always did. Cornelia said that Caleb is crazy, but he pinned her against the wall and said, "I'm fond of Arya too! But I will always choose you over her!"

Cornelia looked worried and said that he has never been this unstable, asking if he's changed because of Julian. "What did Julian do to provoke you?" But Caleb just walked out.

In the meantime, as Arkon walked home, he passed an elderly man pulling a cartful of cardboard. He tried to ignore the man's struggle. Then he decided to try out his powers on the cart. But nothing worked, so he just pushed the cart manually and cracked a smile when the man thanked him.

After a few minutes, Arkon started pulling the cart all by himself as the man loaded it up with more cardboard. Arkon even rolled up his sleeves and helped load cardboard. Then he pulled the heavy cart back to the recycling area.

The old man surprised Arkon by paying him for his help, and he could tell this was the first time Arkon had ever worked. The man told Arkon that it was traditional to buy red long johns for your parents with your first paycheck and advised him that he would gain good fortune!

Arkon took the money and walked. He was delighted as a little child. This was the first real work for the Meridian prince! He stopped at a street vendor when a pair of matching coffee mugs caught his eye, and he remembered that one of Arya's mugs was chipped. He didn't have enough money to buy the mugs, so he offered her to take pictures for him with the mugs in order to model the vendor's wares in exchange. He sure knew how to play to his strengths, and the vendor's girl couldn't believe that there was a human carrying all this beauty.

He spent the afternoon modeling with trinkets while the vendor took photos. He walked away with his coffee mugs, looking pleased with himself.

Meanwhile, Arya's clinic was doing well due to Julian sending all of his friends to her. Arkon called Arya to ask her to meet him, and she smiled when she arrived at the coffee shop and saw him curiously observing all the people.

She went inside and ordered their drinks as Arkon watched her intently. He denied having been curious when Arya bought him one of the drinks he was eyeing, though he complained that she got him a black drink when there were so many other interesting colors of drinks!

Arya accurately nailed his chattering about drinks as nerves because he had something to say to her. He presented her with the coffee mugs, looking so adorably proud of himself, then pretended disinterest in her response.

He told her that he only got them to remind her of her place, which confused her, so he explained the cartoon figures on the mugs. He said the cute pink dragon on one mug is her, wagging her tail happily to see her owner, the handsome man on the other mug that looked like Arkon. He said that it would remind her she belongs to him whenever she used it!

Arya laughed and showed Arkon the other sides of the mugs. On the back of the 'owner' mug was an adorable blue dragon, wagging his tail to see the girl on the 'servant' mug. Arya asked if this meant Arkon would belong to her, and he petulantly tried to take his gift back. "You can't take them back. It's mine," Arya said.

They walked together later, and Arkon proudly told Arya that he worked two jobs to buy the mugs! He showed her pictures of himself carrying cardboard boxes as proof. He even had some of the vendor's extra photos, and he got adorably offended when she pointed out that the stuffed animal he was holding in one shot was the same blue dragon from the mug.

"I have one last patient, so I must go to the clinic," Arya said.

"Okay then, I will go now," Arkon replied.

Julian was Arya's last patient of the day, and she grew worried when he didn't show up or answer her calls. He was at a bar trying to drink away Caleb's threats and hateful words, and by the time he answered his phone, he was good and drunk. He apologized and said he was on his way.

In the meantime, Arkon was also worried, so he called Arya. She said her last client was late, and that was when Julian crashed through the door. She ended the call with Arkon, but not before he heard her say Julian's name.

He was barely conscious, so Arya led him to a chair and checked his temperature. She was afraid to give him medicine because he had so much alcohol, so she took off his jacket and bathed his face and arms with cool water.

Julian was dreaming about his confrontation with Arkon when he'd ripped Julian's shirt open to find the earth guard's mark on his chest. Arya decided to loosen Julian's collar, and Julian woke, imagining her to be Arkon. He lunged at her, imagining that he saw Arkon's face, and he spun her into the chair where he was just sitting as black smoke rose from his hands.

He suddenly snapped out of the daydream, and when he realized that it was Arya, he looked instantly alarmed at what he'd done. He gasped an apology, and Arya watched as a cut on his arm healed in seconds.

Julian was still looming over Arya when Arkon burst into her office. They all froze, and as Arkon and Julian locked gazes, their expressions grew hard.

After a moment of shock, Arkon ran down the stairs to punch Julian. He wanted to punch him again, but Julian caught his arm this time. The two men glared at each other menacingly, but Julian saw Arya looked frightened, so he backed down and offered her an apology. He left, and Arkon stopped Arya from following him with a hand on her arm. She asked Arkon why he went straight to violence without knowing the situation, but he roared that what he saw was pretty obvious!

In Arkon's mind, he interrupted a romantic interlude, and Arya was so offended by his assumption that she refused to tell him what really happened. She asked what they were to each other even to be having this conversation.

That took the fight out of Arkon, and he dropped her hand. Arya stormed out of the office and walked away in the pouring rain, trying not to cry. Equally upset, Arkon stayed in Arya's office all night, fighting back tears of his own.

In the meantime, Arya's friend Nani woke from where she had fallen asleep in her odd little booth, sensing that Arya was on her way. Sure enough, when she came out, Arya was there, dripping wet and looking utterly bereft.

"What happened? Why are you covered with rain?" Nani asked.

"Can I sleep in your home today?" Arya asked.

Nani asked, "What happened? Is everything all right?" Arya started to cry, and her voice broke when she said she didn't want to go home.

Julian spent the night in his office, and he woke from more nightmares featuring Arya and killing flowers with a touch, and his tiny friend, the blind girl, planting flowers for him. The last flash was of something that looked like bodies lying on the ground. That was what woke him up, and he jumped in terror to find the magical servant Herbert standing beside him. Julian sighed and remembered that he called Herbert last night when he was walking in the rain. He reminded Herbert that he once said that it wasn't Julian's fault he was born with such terrible power and asked if Herbert only said that because he was afraid of him. Herbert looked haunted. "Who was responsible for all the deaths I caused in the past, if not me!" Julian started crying and said, "Since these immortals appeared in my life again, I began to lose my confidence and all the good life that I had built in this world. They remind me about my old self after I forgot everything and started to live a good life."

In Arya's clinic, Matt was surprised to see the clinic's door open early. He thought that Arya had come early, but he found Arkon still in the office and nearly died of fright before he realized who it was. Arkon said calmly that he was waiting, but his eyes flickered uncertainly when Arya showed up behind Matt with Nani on the stairs.

Arya asked Arkon why he didn't go home, and he said that he couldn't, though he wasn't exactly waiting for her. He explained that he fell asleep while trying to think of a way out of the office! He tried to leave, but he couldn't lock the door behind himself. He ended up staying all night rather than leaving the office unlocked, which would be irresponsible of him. He played it off like he was irritated that Arya left without locking up, and he insisted that he stayed because he was thinking of others. Also, he chided Arya for selfishly leaving without giving him the key, then magnanimously forgave her. "Don't worry if you feel sorry now; I forgive you!"

"Oh, thanks for your great grace!" Arya replied sarcastically. Then she said, "Please, let's get out of here."

He stood and approached her, staring into her eyes, and said softly, "I want to be irresponsible; I don't want that. I don't want to care about anything. You asked me for a definition for our relationship; I want you to know that you are not a distant sound that will fade, nor are you insignificant."

His voice grew soft, then he said, "I want to hold you and kiss you. I want you to be my beginning and my end. I want my mind to be filled with thoughts of you. I want my jealousy to be justified, and I don't want to feel guilty after punching someone."

He added, "For that to happen, I have to begin. I know our future is predestined, but may I begin?"

Arya listened to his confession, and tears were welling in her eyes. Then she gave her answer: "No, don't begin."

In Caleb's penthouse, Cornelia woke up to find Caleb making coffee; she had been staying at his place like Arkon told her to. Caleb said he envied humans for their ability to get drunk because he couldn't manage it despite drinking until dawn. He wondered about the weaknesses of humans and snapped his fingers to produce a huge diamond ring, pointing out how something like this doesn't impress Cornelia. She stated, "Don't begin, please."

"What are your plans for today?" Caleb asked.

"Well, I have nothing to do today except keep my eyes on you!" Cornelia replied.

He liked that idea. Then he spent the day jogging and working out, leaving Cornelia excruciatingly bored and fending off male admirers at the gym.

She saw Caleb's constant shadow, Menar, and asked him, "Why do you never speak? Did I really freeze and crush your tongue in the past?" Menar just stared at her and spoke no word. Eventually, Cornelia demanded to know why Caleb was so anxious today, but he refused to tell her. So she asked what he wanted from Julian, and the question wiped the smile off Caleb's face. He simply said, "I want him to die." Cornelia promptly called her manager and canceled her schedule for the rest of the day, but Caleb smirked that he'd just forgotten about Julian for today.

In Julian's office, Julian sat, remembering his conversation with Herbert, when Herbert suggested that Julian tell Arya about everything and ask for help. Julian told him he was not sure that she saw his arm cut heal, but Julian told him Arya is an immortal's servant, and she is the most qualified human to understand him. Meanwhile, Chairman Hale entered the office with his granddaughter

Miranda. He demanded to know if he was engaged to Arya or if she knew his weakness, figuring that was the only reason Julian would decide not to buy her land. He was mainly angry that he didn't own land in the new area where the mall was being built, meaning he wouldn't stand to profit.

But he pretended it was a concern for Julian, and he began to lay on the guilt trip by talking about how he took care of him. But Julian cut him off and said he had a meeting, telling Chairman Hale firmly that he wouldn't be changing his mind about the new mall's location.

In the meantime, Arkon was on the rooftop, indulged because Arya had rejected him. "She rejected me! A human girl rejected the great prince of Meridian. I haven't felt like this in my whole life." He got himself all worked up, wailing that she didn't know whom she turned down. He called her stupid and dense, and then sighed that she was also cowardly.

He called Caleb, asking for his help in losing his iron control for once. Caleb was up for the challenge, but Cornelia was upset, just thinking about why Arkon would want to lose control. She asked Caleb why Arkon would call him when he didn't even like him, and he explained that it was because he was a guy! Before he went there, Cornelia warned him to just hang out with Arkon and not get into trouble, so Caleb promised to behave. Then he added thoughtfully, "I always listen to you."

Caleb took Arkon to a bar, hoping alcohol would work better on Arkon than it does on him. Arkon eyed the shot of liquor suspiciously, but Caleb promised this was the way to lose control, so he drank it down. Chuckling to himself, Caleb asked if things weren't going well with Arya, but Arkon just took another shot. Caleb talked about Arya, whom he knew from college, whom he described as looking 'like freesias in spring'. He said she wore short skirts and dated a lot, which spurred Arkon to take several more shots. When Caleb said that he tried to give Arya a diamond ring, but she refused it, Arkon started chugging from the bottle.

After a short while, they got out of the bar, and Arkon started talking with a mailbox. Caleb began to record Arkon with his phone, and he was still recording later as a very drunk Arkon discussed being rejected by a human girl with a mailbox. A group of men wandered by and started harassing Arkon. They grabbed at him and told him to give them his wallet.

Despite the alcohol, Arkon was still his usual arrogant self, and it was not long before a fight broke out. At first, Caleb just watched him, enjoying the show, but then he snapped his fingers, leaving his camera still recording while hanging in midair. Then he jumped in to bash some heads.

In the meantime, in Arya's office, she was shaken by Arkon's confession. She imagined him sitting in her office, looking at her with disappointment. She heard him again in her head, asking her if he should begin. She said to herself that no matter how many times she thinks about it, her answer will still be no.

When she finally left the clinic for home, Julian was following her at a short distance, thinking about following Herbert's advice and telling her the truth about himself. He thought about his vow to win her fairly, but then he remembered how he nearly killed her last night, so he hesitated, wondering if he deserves her.

Meanwhile, Tynar called Arya to ask her to tell Arkon that he got a chicken delivery job and won't be home until very late. Then she got a call from Julian, who assured her that he was fine after what happened last night. She didn't realize that he was right behind her as she walked, and she offered apologies on Arkon's behalf. She kept the conversation to impersonal topics, and Julian soon stopped following her and ended the call. When she arrived at her home, it was just a moment until Caleb came and delivered the mostly unconscious Arkon to Arya. He draped him over her like a scarf. He wondered aloud if, if he asked Arya for a favor, he should ask her to keep Arkon here or let him go. He decided he didn't know how he felt and should probably book a session with Arya at the clinic, then left with a wry smile on his face.

Arya struggled to carry Arkon in his state, so she somehow got him inside, intending to let him stay until Tynar returned. Arkon tripped on the stairs and took Arya down with him, landing on top of her on the floor. It took some effort for Arya to get out from under Arkon, and once she did, she stopped to catch her breath. She sneaked a peek at his sleeping face. She started to remove his arm from her waist, but he just pulled her closer. He said softly, with his eyes still closed, "Let's just stay like this. I won't begin, so don't be afraid. Just stay for a few minutes."

His hand moved up from Arya's waist until it found her hand, and he held on tightly. Arya looked at Arkon for a long time. Then she moved her other hand on top of his. She closed her eyes, and they both drifted off to sleep!

The next day, at Caleb's penthouse, Cornelia watched Caleb's recordings of Arkon, shocked to see him behaving so out of character. She wondered why Arkon hadn't gone back to ask about the jewel yet, and although Caleb looked like he knew something, he just said that Arkon was trying things out before the duties of his throne weighed him down.

In the meantime, Arya woke in her own bed, and she got up to find Arkon gone. Then he wandered up the stairs with his coffee and a book like he did every morning, and he asked her about the books in her house. She said that they are mostly travel books and that she hasn't read the one he was holding, which was titled *Black Swan*.

She looked at the sunlight and said, "Oh, I should hang laundry."

Taking Arkon's cue, Arya acted as if nothing had happened between them. She asked Arkon to read the first line of his book to her while she hung laundry, saying that she can tell if she wants to read a book just by hearing the first line. He balked, but he finally read it, with her insistence, the first sentence, which seemed to describe their relationship perfectly! Arya said, "That doesn't sound good. Read me something else from the middle of the book or read me the end of it." Arkon turned the pages and read.

"I believe in destiny; now I believe that our love was destined, but our separation and our problems were personal choices. Love and confess your love to those you love. Life will not wait for you. Do not postpone. You do not know what happened tomorrow. You may regret things you did not do. You can make the ends happy, but what about the beginnings? A day passes by. A day becomes past or an imagination. What do you want? What do you become? This is the question."

Arya felt very attracted to the words. He continued for a few more sentences. Both of them grew more emotional over the beautiful words. Just as he read a line about not wanting to ascribe their miraculous connection to fate, Arya stopped him. She said lightly, "I like the book. The words are pure and fine. Now come; let's go inside and eat." Once she was downstairs, Arya wiped away a single tear before going inside.

She made the breakfast for them and used the couple cups that Arkon bought for her. Arkon eyeballed his breakfast; he asked Arya if it was edible, and she watched him anxiously as he took a bite. He looked like he was trying to eat without actually letting the food touch his tongue. He said, "Congratulations; it can be eaten."

He suddenly asked Arya why she used to wear miniskirts and date a lot and why she doesn't look like freesias in spring anymore! Caleb had told Arya that he told Arkon she was innocent and ladylike, which she now knew was a bald-faced lie. She turned it around on Arkon, saying that he's probably dated countless women in his long life! She asked which one he liked the most, but he just clammed up and shoved more food into his mouth.

Arkon told Arya that he'd have paid her back by now if he had his powers, so she asked what he would have done. He said he'd fix the things she broke and make it so she can swim and drink cold water. Arya replied that she could do those things herself, challenging him to think of a better repayment. She offered some suggestions, like making it find gold on her land or making her an oil field's owner or building her a house that looked like a cathedral on some island and make her prettier. Arkon said, "I can do everything you said, except make you prettier because even the most immortals' beauty can't be like yours!"

Arya's cheeks went red upon hearing that. She continued with her outlandish requests, getting more and more creative, like having tea with the Queen of England, and when she finally winded down, she realized that Arkon had left the table. He quipped dryly that human emotions are confusing and annoying, but Arya told him that a king should listen to his people.

As she made him coffee, Arkon said things would be different if she had the servant's tablet, which has the power to fulfill one of the servant's wishes. Arya said, "Well, give it!"

Arkon replied, "Actually, it's with the guards, and it was with Van that day when he lost his memories nine years ago!"

He explained that he wouldn't have been able to grant her wish to live on an island anyway because it has to be for something she truly wants. Before she could ask more questions, Tynar arrived, and he proudly showed off the money he earned before heading down to eat breakfast.

Tynar noticed Arya's cute matching mugs, and she said that Arkon bought them for her after working a part-time job. Tynar was scandalized at the idea of the prince working a lowly job, and he flounced off to the roof in a full-on sulk. Arkon followed him, but he stomped off, angry and hurt! While Arkon started himself a bubble bath, Arya asked if he wanted to go see the ocean. She mentioned that he could look up how to make lunchboxes, and though he was initially indignant at the idea of doing it himself, her threat to take the breakfast leftovers instead had him quickly pulling out his phone, and he searched on the way to make a picnic basket.

He decided on an array of fancy foods, all of which Arya nixed in favor of pasta. They worked on assembling the food side by side, and Arkon watched

Arya incredulously as she proceeded to reduce her Swiss rolls to shreds. Meanwhile, Cornelia called him to invite him to lunch with her and Caleb. He turned her down. "I can't because I'm going to the beach." He snapped at Arya for hacking at her Swiss rolls with a knife. So he hung up on Cornelia, leaving her completely confused.

Jealousy took control of Cornelia. She picked up Caleb's phone to watch the videos of Arkon again. She found one she hadn't seen before, and as she watched it, her eyes went wide. It was a recording of Arkon at the bar, very drunk, as he was saying, "If only I could, I would live with that woman here in this world." She immediately drove to Arya's house at top speed, screaming Arkon's name.

On the roof, Arya packed up her torn Swiss rolls as Arkon tried to call Tynar. They heard steps on the stairs, but it was not Tynar—it was the veil guard, Cornelia, who stalked towards Arya angrily.

She approached Arya and yelled, "Do you know why a lowly human like you is even allowed to speak to immortals? I wonder if you would be able to stay near Arkon if you knew the truth about your ancestor!"

Ignoring Arkon's yelling and objections, Cornelia said, "I'm going to show you how your ancestor ended up as the immortals' servant." She grabbed Arya's hand, and the two of them disappeared into thin air, leaving Arkon shouting after her futilely.

Chapter Nine
The Tale of the Ancestor

On the top roof of a skyscraper, Cornelia and Arya stood, and Cornelia started to tell the story of Arya's ancestor.

"There was a young woman called Tylen; she was sacrificial for human greed. When Arkon saw her on Vision Lake, he ordered the servant to protect her, so they took her to the great world of Meridian, and she was the first human to enter Meridian, but after long years living in grace and the greatness of our world, she betrayed Arkon, so the queen ordered to put her in a cave and ordered to kill her, and Caleb asked the queen to make all the ancestry of that woman servants for the immortals on earth. On that day, the woman was captured. Arkon visited her in the cave…"

MERIDIAN, 2850 YEARS AGO

Arkon entered the dark cave, and he conjured blue water fireflies to light his way, and Caleb followed him hesitantly.

With a wave of his hand, Arkon revealed the watery barrier that caged Tylen, who was bound and asleep. He spoke her name, and she woke, and he could hear her calling his name in her mind. Arkon told Tylen that Queen Wera had ordered her execution. He said she would gain the eternal life she coveted, existing in a never-ending limbo, forbidden to either move on to the next world or be reincarnated in this one. Tylen begged Arkon to have pity and save her, but he just looked at her coldly and said, "I will never forgive you."

Tylen was taken to the edge of the sea, where Queen Wera and Caleb waited to witness her execution. Arkon thought about when he and Tylen were in love as Cornelia stood nearby. Tylen was led to the very edge of the ocean, and Queen Wera waved a hand, conjuring a force that took over Tylen's body. Tylen screamed Arkon's name as she walked into the water against her will, futilely begging for her life until the very end.

At the moment of Tylen's death, he bowed his head in sorrow. Cornelia covered him with his cloak, and Arkon had one last vision of Tylen admiring a flower. He picked it up and threw it into the ocean, where she had died.

Cornelia told Arya that Tylen's life wasn't enough to appease Queen Wera, who also demanded the lives of her brother and his son. The brother begged for mercy, vowing in exchange that he and his descendants would serve the immortals forever. After she finished the story, Arya replied, "What should that mean to me? What is the relation between my ancestors and me? Even if one of my parents killed or stole, why is that related to me? Should I feel guilty for what that woman did? Sorry, I can't feel that." Cornelia told her that she's foolish and doesn't fully understand. In the meantime, Arkon paced Arya's house until she came home, and when she did, she made light of the situation and brushed off his concern. Arkon demanded to know what Cornelia said to her, so Arya said, "She didn't say much; she told me about your past and your old love story, and actually, I didn't find it interesting."

She asked why she should be responsible for something her ancestor did very long ago, calling it ridiculous. Upset, Arkon asked her if that was really what Arya wanted to say, and Arya looked him right in the eye and told him, "Go back; go where you belong as soon as possible." He growled that he'd leave when he pleased; then he turned to go. But Arya said to his back, "You did nothing. When the woman you loved was dying, you did nothing!" Arkon glared at Arya and stormed out, slamming the door behind him.

He didn't know that Cornelia told Arya to make Arkon leave, whatever it took. She'd told Arya that Arkon is hesitating to go home because he's in love with her, so she has to make him go. Cornelia had explained that Arkon and the realm of Meridian are inextricably linked, so no matter what he wants, he has to go back and ask where to find the jewel and be the next king.

Also, she told her that Arkon punished himself when Tylen died, and she can't stand to see that again. She'd earnestly begged Arya not to hold him back as Tylen did.

Back at Caleb's penthouse, Cornelia told Caleb that she wished she could cry, get drunk, or do any of the stupid things humans do. "I'm angry, and this anger drives me crazy. I admitted in front of her that he was in love with her. Why should this be the only way to send him back?" Cornelia stated.

Caleb replied, "You did what you should do; don't regret it. There is no reason to feel angry." He gave her a back hug and said he would beat Arkon up if she'd let him.

Neither Arkon nor Arya could sleep that night. On the next morning, Arkon dressed in the suit he had worn when he came to this country, and he looked at the door between his room and Arya's roof, though he didn't go through it. He stepped outside and woke Tynar, asking him if his feelings were hurt when Arkon worked to buy Arya a present. Tynar admitted it, and Arkon apologized! And he said that he knew Tynar worked hard at multiple jobs while Arkon just took baths and enjoyed food and books.

Tynar loudly begged forgiveness for being upset with him, but Arkon added, "You weren't actually expecting me to say such things, were you?"

They went down to breakfast, where Arkon actually thanked Arya for the meal. He handed over his and Tynar's phones and asked Arya to cancel the service and dispose of his clothes and books! He told Arya not to stay out late and to get a porch light that turns on automatically after dark. He instructed her to eat better, clean the house more, and submit a complaint when the streetlight out front isn't working so she doesn't have to walk home in the dark. Arkon dismissed Tynar, and once they were alone, he reminded Arya that he could see it on her face when she lies. But he said that last night he couldn't tell, and he realized that she truly wanted him to leave. He admitted that he bluffed that he would protect her and that he was embarrassed that he made a promise he knew he couldn't keep.

"Will you be okay if I leave? What do you really feel?" Arkon asked in misery.

"I will be okay," Arya replied, and tears poured from her eyes. Her heart was squeezing from the inside, but she held on to her power. She blinked back tears. "I'll barely notice you have left, other than a bit of loneliness. Don't forget, I'm good at enduring since I'm only third-rate," Arya stated.

She said, "Can I drive you to the gate?"

Arkon stared at her and replied, "No, there is no need to do that. Let's separate here." He opened the door and got out of the house, and Tynar with Caleb was outside, waiting for him. Arya followed him, and tears filled her eyes.

Tynar bowed and said, "Take care of yourself; goodbye." And he followed Arkon out of the iron gate. When they left, Arya looked at the sky and started to cry heavily.

At the gate, Arkon stared back to take one last long look at this world. He heard Arya's voice through the air saying, "Goodbye…goodbye." Then he stepped through the gate back to the world of Meridian.

At her clinic, Arya was aggressively cheerful all day, and Matt noticed how manic Arya seemed, but she just griped that he was too negative. Nani burst in to confront Arya, upset that she asked a friend to set her up with someone. Arya's excessive laughter made Nani and Matt worry, so Nani took Arya out for coffee. She squinted suspiciously as Arya insisted, a bit too brightly, that she was not as broken up about Arkon's leaving as she thought she'd be! She babbled on and on about how very okay she was until Nani blew up and said she was happy they broke up, but she was not glad to see that Arya wasn't crying. She reminded Arya that she used to brag about how good she was at enduring pain, but Arya ended the conversation.

Arya headed back to her office, where Julian was waiting for his session.

When Arya returned, they both apologized for what happened the night he showed up drunk in her office. She said, "I know that it was reacting to a bad dream, and I want to ask you what happened that reminded you of the past that you hate?"

Julian hesitated, then finally said, "I met some people I never wanted to meet."

"As I have told you before, you must try to think about something else, and I know that it's not easy, but what do you say if we try this? You said that you experienced something that reminded you of your past. Can you tell me what that thing is?" Arya asked.

He remained silent, so Arya added, "Is that hard too?" He told Arya that those people want to lock him up in his past, criticize him, and remind him of what he used to be. Arya said kindly that nobody can change their past and ended their session when Julian didn't appear to want to talk about it any further, though she added that he should trust her more. Julian shook off his dark mood and asked Arya to have dinner with him. She hesitated since he was technically a patient, but he talked her into it. At the restaurant, Julian jokingly admitted that he was still miffed. She tried to push him away when he simply wanted to have dinner and be friends. He started listing off all the things he knew about Arya—her financial situation, her personality, whom she likes, why she was hurting right now—though he assured her that he never stalked her; he just has a photographic memory. He added that she also knew a lot about him and comforted and encouraged him, too.

It was his way of pointing out that they were entirely qualified to be friends, and Julian listed all of his positive attributes and sighed that he was not asking her to marry him or anything, which made her laugh. Then he held out a hand, and Arya shook it, sealing their agreement to be friends. At that moment, Cornelia and Caleb walked into the restaurant and saw them. Caleb glowered and stared toward Julian, but Cornelia stopped him. She told him just to leave quietly, so he did, ordering Menar to take Cornelia home and driving off alone! Cornelia asked Menar, "Why is Caleb behaving like this around Julian?" But, of course, Menar didn't say a word.

After dinner, Julian and Arya went for a walk, and he said he was still a tiny bit miffed because he doesn't ask many people to be his friend. She laughed at his ability to hold a grudge and said she was a little miffed herself since he doesn't trust her as his psychiatrist. Arya turned to see a street vendor's table, and she recognized the blue stuffed dinosaur from Arkon's modeling pictures. Julian offered to buy the dinosaur for her, unaware of its significance, but Arya jumped in and paid for the dinosaur herself.

Julian got a call from work. He said, "I'm sorry because I will have to let you go home alone; I have something urgent to do." She walked home by herself. She stared at the house, and it was not her home. It was back again, pale and full of loneliness. She made coffee and drank it from Arkon's mug, the one with the matching blue dinosaur. Then she went upstairs to his empty roof room. She thought about the times they spent together, then saw the book he'd read to her, *Black Swan.*

She reread the part he'd read aloud to her. "I didn't want to think that we met by mere coincidence. So the only thing I can do is do my best." That was where she'd cut him off, but today she continued on. "…To love you. At this moment, I am passing through your love." As she read, Arya's tears fell on the pages. Finally, she gave in and sobbed, heartbroken.

In the world of Meridian, Arkon was flying over everything—every cloud, waterfall, and tree. He couldn't believe that he was able to use his powers again. He flew to the king's palace, but he saw his mother, Queen Wera, walking back from the Lake of Visions. He landed on the ground, and the queen saw him and opened her arms wide for a hug. He approached her and hugged her.

"My prince, my little boy!" Queen said.

"My queen, I missed you so much. There are many things I would like to say—" Arkon replied.

But the queen interrupted and said, "I know; I saw everything!"

"That means you know that I didn't find the jewel," Arkon replied.

"Yes, I know; your father knows too," Queen Wera replied.

"I'm sorry; I really don't know what the reason is behind that. I came to see if you both knew what I should do."

The queen said, "We can't bring the jewel back with our powers once it is on earth, so you must find it yourself…"

The next day, on earth, Arya wasn't in such a good mood. She imagined Arkon sitting in her office, gently chiding her for saying she's okay when she's not. She replied that she was the one who broke up with him, but he said that it feels like the other way around! He guessed that she hated him for not catching her lie and said that it's impossible never to hurt anyone. He told her that lots of people live certain moments as if that day were their last because they know they need to live today in order to see tomorrow, and they believe that memory will last them the rest of their lives.

Imaginary Arkon asked Arya if that was not easier than trying to find a way never to hurt anyone. Arya let out a wry little laugh and whispered that he was not even human, and Arkon faded away.

Nani looked up to see Arya standing in front of her, dripping wet, in Nani's shop. She fussed at Arya for never carrying an umbrella, but Arya just silently mouthed something to her friend, then turned to the door. Someone else walked in, but all Nani saw were a pair of shoes, also soaking wet, before Nani woke up with a start. She tasked that Arya must still be in love with that immortal. Then she called Arya and told her to come see her when she could, to tell her about this weird dream.

In the meantime, in Julian's office, Cornelia sat in front of him. She revealed, "Arkon left this world; he went to the great world of Meridian, but who told you? The servant? Oh, a lovely woman; she wants you as a replacement, right?"

Julian barked, "Don't you dare talk about Miss Arya in that way in front of me!"

"Okay, I'm not here to argue. I'm here because I have something to tell you. I want you to take care of Arya! No, actually, I want you to make her your own," Cornelia stated.

"What are you trying to do? Are you trying to be responsible?" Julian asked.

"Actually, I don't care about her. I only want you to make her forget the prince, and I want you to take her away from him because maybe he will come back!" Cornelia replied.

Julian said, "I can't do that easily."

Cornelia replied, "Try, just try. However, you wanted to do that anyway, right? And marry her and stay with her until she dies, because this is the only way to cut the connection between us."

"Even if I'm planning to do that, I will not take the orders from you. Please leave my office right now!" Julian roared.

Meanwhile, Arya went up to Nani's booth as she requested, and Nani offered to read Arya's fortune, which she had never done before. But a frantic call from Matt had Arya rushing back to her office, where she found Chairman Hale's representative with several men packing up her things. He told Arya that Chairman Hale wasn't willing to wait any longer for the rent, and he refused to accept the money from her today. He passed on the message that this decision was Miranda's, who held the real power.

In the meantime, Arya's patient, Salar, the man Arkon saved from drowning and whose father ran the bank, showed up for his appointment and ordered the men to stop in a booming, authoritative voice. He stood in front of Arya protectively and told them to put everything back, but then he lost control and started swinging with both fists. The room erupted into pandemonium, and Salar was still fighting later, as they were all at the police station making their statements. Arya was in a bit of a fix, not having anyone to call to act as her guarantor. While Arya was in a big mess, Julian showed up, having been called by Matt. He settled everything, and Nani with Matt took Salar home.

Alone with Arya, Julian admitted that he laughed a bit when he got the call because she'd been so leery of being friends but had to call him then.

He offered her a ride home, but Arya said she'd take a walk to clear her head. Julian said he would call her later to make sure she got home okay. Then she headed off alone.

Julian called while she was still walking, and he was following her on foot, making sure she was safe. Arya told him that she just learned that her building owner's granddaughter was her old school nemesis. She complained that she didn't know why Miranda hated her so much, and Julian sympathized, saying that he was dealing with people like that too. Julian offered to go with Arya to talk to her landlord or even to buy the building!

Arya turned the corner to her alley, then stopped dead in her tracks. She dropped her phone in shock as she saw the prince of Meridian, Arkon, waiting for her under the yellow streetlight, like he had never left. Arya took a tentative step toward him, then another, then broke into a run and threw herself into his arms. Arkon caught her and held her tight as she sobbed. He whispered, "I told you to come home early. You really don't listen to me!"

Up the street, Julian was worried when Arya didn't answer him. He turned the corner and saw her in Arkon's arms, so he ducked back behind the wall where they couldn't spot him.

Arkon sweetly fussed at Arya for looking thin and tired, then joked that if she'd looked like freesias in spring, he'd have gone right back. He wiped away her tears. Arkon reminded her that he had warned her that there was no medicine for that if she fell in love with him. He headed up the hill to retrieve Arya's dropped phone, bringing him within mere feet of Julian's hiding place, but Arkon didn't see him. Julian watched again as Arkon led Arya home, and their arms were around each other.

Tynar was thrilled to see Arya, and she fed him dinner and asked why they were back. While they sat at the table, Arkon said, "Queen Wera told me that I must find the jewel and I have limited time to find it, or I will be forced to go back to Meridian and wait for the jewel's comeback by itself in a thousand years. She told me that the jewel is related to the heir. She said I must use my heart to find it because I must show my deepest desire to make it appear. I must wear the crown soon, so I must find it in a short period of time, but I don't know how I will do that without my powers. Even if I have my powers, I will not be able to use them on the jewel. The queen explained that my power is related to the jewel, and I would not be able to use it here without finding the jewel, but she said something I couldn't understand. She said that I must see the purest desire inside me to see the light of the jewel, and I must look where I do not expect to look."

He left the table and went upstairs. Then Arya followed him and found him scowling at her blue stuffed dinosaur. He accused Arya of using a toy to meet her emotional needs, abusing it while she took her anger out on it. Then he cuddled the dinosaur close and asked if she was so lonely at night that she did something weird to it instead! Arya grabbed the dinosaur and made Arkon grin with satisfaction. Then he headed to the door to his rooftop apartment, which Arya had never let him use before, and he asked why she insisted on going a long way when there was a much faster way. They both smiled at his double meaning.

Arkon stepped through and complained that it hadn't been cleaned while he was gone, gently berating Arya for not eating well and not canceling his phone contract. He said that she never does what he tells her. Then he asked how she really had been. Arya turned her back to him and asked why he really came back, and Arkon crossed the room and folded her into a back hug. Then he whispered into her ear, "I came because I knew you weren't doing well. I have to go back. Going back is my path, as it always has been. I came to say goodbye properly. I want to love without any regrets. Even if we have to separate, I want to love enough that I can understand why we're parting!"

He said that if Arya wasn't ready or disagreed, then he'd go back. She said that making sure they've loved enough to say goodbye doesn't make any sense, and yet it sounds nice. "When I think about the past, I find that I didn't love myself. Who would fall in love with me when even I didn't love myself? There must be someone who took pity on me that I have luck today with you," Arya said.

Arkon turned her and stared at her face, then he said, "That because you are a good human."

"I'm not a good human," Arya replied.

"No, you are!" Arkon insisted.

"Well, I'm not going to argue with you, but, as you lived here for a little while, I think you realized by now that no one living in this world would be totally good. Now if I believe what you said, it means that every good person meets a respectful man like you, right?" Arya said.

"Well, I'm not a human! I'm an immortal and the next king of the great world of Meridian."

"Okay, every good human will meet the king of Meridian. Is that what I should learn?" She smiled while she was staring into his eyes.

Arkon asked, "Is that enough?" She asked what else she gets, and Arkon told her, "This," then leaned down and kissed her. After a minute, Arkon pulled back to gauge Arya's reaction, but she just looked up at him with wide eyes, so he kissed her again.

Outside, Julian watched Arya's house for a while. He remembered Cornelia telling him to make Arya his own, and as he leaned against the wall that has Arkon and Arya's names written on it, he said to himself that's not something he can make happen just because he wants it.

In the morning, when Arya didn't find Arkon in his room like usual, her face fell, perhaps wondering if she had imagined last night. Then she ran outside and was relieved to find Tynar and Arkon having a normal morning. Tynar asked why Arya was coming out of Arkon's room, and she stammered that she was looking for something. Arkon asked, "Were you looking for me?" He walked past her to go inside. It completely flustered Arya, which made Arkon laugh.

They gathered in the house, where Arya surprised the guys by saying that her clinic was closed for the near future because of the landlord. But she said cheerfully that she lives with an immortal prince with magical powers, so she could benefit from his extraordinary abilities for now. Arkon looked away awkwardly as Tynar explained that he still doesn't have his powers back. Arya was shocked, so Arkon said his powers came back when he went home, but he left them behind again to come back here.

In the meantime, Caleb was swimming while Cornelia napped by the pool. He woke her when her phone rang, advising her to be nicer to her manager, who was calling. Cornelia glared at Caleb, but she softened her tone with the manager, who tearfully thanked Caleb for convincing her director to reshoot the twice-doomed kissing scene!

Caleb told Cornelia that he disagreed with the saying that no person lives for another because he lived for her. She asked sarcastically if that was why he left for eight years. Caleb wondered if she missed him, and Cornelia's halting denial gave her away. He laughed and noted that their lives are extremely peaceful when Arkon's not around and since he left. She tried to leave past him, but he stopped her and offered his help to practice kissing. He kissed her soundly, and when she pushed him away, he told her to remember that feeling. Cornelia aimed a slap at him, but he dodged it, then caught her arm on the second swing.

Still wearing her lipstick, Caleb reminded Cornelia that he was her fiancé, reminding her that she begged him to tell Arkon they were engaged because she was jealous of his girl. Caleb said that he even broke up with the prettiest immortal girl of the Meridian realm because of it, and that Arkon congratulated them and didn't care as she had wished. When Cornelia tried to slap him a third time, he caught her and turned it into a hug. As he struggled to hang onto the thrashing Cornelia, Caleb asked why she pretended not to know his feelings for her. She stopped struggling, and he backed away, and when she tried again to slap him, he asked her not to hit him because it hurt.

In Julian's office, Herbert found Julian sleeping in his office and asked if this was about Arya. Julian just apologized for being a bother and promised it wouldn't happen again. Herbert stopped him in his tracks by mentioning that he didn't want to do it when his immortal father ordered him to take Julian from his mother and lock him away in that cave.

Herbert said he tried to ignore the tiny infant and waited for Julian to die, but he felt bad for the lonely little boy. He admitted that he was torn between saving and abandoning Julian and that he tried not to become attached. Herbert said that he came to the human world to avoid Julian, but it didn't work, and that cave and Julian were always in his heart. He reached up and pulled off his hair to reveal that he's bald on top, and he said wryly that even in the human world, beggars have to look good.

Julian smiled and said that Herbert looked better like this. Herbert advised Julian to show Arya who he really was, and if she still doesn't accept him, then they're not meant to be together.

Arkon went to see Cornelia and Caleb in Caleb's penthouse. They were extremely unhappy that he was back, though, for different reasons. Cornelia was too angry to talk, so Arkon took Caleb to a nearby café and explained.

"What are you both expecting from me? I must find the jewel to make the inauguration."

"This concerned Cornelia," Caleb said.

"I know what bothers her, but I have nothing to do about that," Arkon replied.

"Okay, then just behave without making her go mad."

"I must think very carefully, and I must think about many things," Arkon replied.

"Don't say that you will not go back to Meridian. You know very well what would happen to you if you did not go back."

"Don't worry; I will go back," Arkon asserted.

"Why isn't Cornelia enough for you?" Caleb asked.

Arkon immediately responded, "Don't insult her with that. I know that you don't mean that. Why don't you go and care about your personal business instead of this?"

"I hoped that hate was allowed in Meridian. You would be my first enemy, Your Highness!" Caleb stated.

"I will consider making it allowed when I take the throne," Arkon said wryly.

Caleb left his chair angrily. When he got out of the restaurant's door, he saw Arya come in. He stopped her and said, "Are you okay? I didn't know that you were not smart like that! I want you to know that I'm not on your side, and obviously not on Arkon's. I will only do what Cornelia wants me to do. I did that to your family in the first place, do you know why? Because Cornelia was angry because of that woman whom Arkon loved thousands of years ago, so I convinced the queen to make them servants, so you can pray that Cornelia will not be as mad as the last time, because I don't know what I will do."

He walked away, and Arya was confused. She ignored him, entered the café, and walked toward Arkon's table. She found Arkon, who was grumpy because Caleb and Cornelia refused his request for a new car.

Arkon asked, "What did you talk with that idiot about for a long time?"

"Nothing; he just wanted to bother me," Arya replied.

They took their coffee and went for a walk. "I'm blessed that they didn't give you a new car," Arya stated.

"Yes, they didn't give me a car, but I ordered Caleb to find me a car!" Arkon replied.

"Will he obey you?" Arya asked.

Arkon replied, "I'm still the prince." Then he got a call and shot Arya a triumphant smirk, crowing that Caleb had found him a car.

In the meantime, Cornelia went to see Julian in his office. When she arrived there, she saw Herbert leaving his office. She asked Julian, "Do you know him?"

But he didn't answer her and replied to her with a question: "What are you doing here?"

"Arkon is back, as I told you before," Cornelia said.

"I know," Julian replied.

"How did you know? Oh, I think you caught them together. How did you find them? Were they kissing each other?" She went silent, then continued, "Forget it. Listen to me; the war starts now, and I'm on your side!"

"Are you beside me?" Julian asked, hesitating.

"Yes, the greatest guard and the most powerful immortal in Meridian support you! If you do not win her heart, you shall take it with power! Do whatever you can to take Arya and to separate her from Arkon."

Julian laughed and said, "Use power! Do you think I may use power on innocent humans like Arya? Also, I heard that your future king is powerless here without the Jewel of Meridian, and you should be afraid because if he comes in my way, I may hurt him. Also, I don't need your help, and if you and your friend Caleb will use your powers for him, I will use mine too! So let's not do that for each other because using my powers in the realm of humans is one of the things that I hate very much."

When Cornelia became angry, Caleb opened the office door and rushed in. When Cornelia saw him, she said, "Time to leave." She stumbled, and Julian steadied her with a hand on her arm, but Caleb immediately sucker-punched him just for touching her. "Don't you ever again dare to touch her," Caleb said.

Then he snarled that he was holding his temper because Cornelia had asked him to, and he warned Julian to stay out of his sight. He held Cornelia's arm and left the office. In the parking garage, she yelled at him to leave her arm and said, "I was only talking with him, then he caught my hand because I was about to fall. What's wrong with you?"

"Don't talk to him. He's not one of us," Caleb replied.

"Even so, I understand that you hate him, but why are you doing this? Can you just ignore him, like he does not exist? Are you doing that because you fear him?" Cornelia replied. Then her facial expressions changed, and she continued, "Your eyes are full of hate and anger; you hide something, and until I know the real reason behind that, I can't accept your actions." He refused to explain further, and he accused Cornelia of hanging around Julian to make Arkon jealous. Also, he offered to seduce Arya to clear Cornelia's path to Arkon, and this time, Cornelia slapped him hard. "Idiot, you will never understand my feelings," Cornelia stated.

Caleb drove away angrily, and Cornelia called for Menar, whom she knew would be nearby. She ordered him to tell her why Caleb was acting like this, and he spoke to her for the first time. "It's because of me! And that's what all I can tell you, my lady."

In the meantime, Arkon took Arya for a ride in his new car, and they went back home. Sitting on the table with matching coffee cups, Arya said, "Are you sad? Don't worry. We can do that on another day; you were so excited, so I had to prevent you from driving on the highway because I don't want to die! Also, I just wanted to sit like this and stare at you; that's enough for me. Is this real? Am I dreaming? If this is a dream, I don't want to wake up."

Arkon put his hand out and touched her cheeks. Then she closed her eyes and laid her face on his hand. Then she said, "This is real." She stayed like that for a moment; then she raised her head, and her cheeks were red. Arya suggested they drive to see the sunset tomorrow.

Arkon repeated, "Sunset?"

Arya said, "Sunrise and sunset, people here go to specific places to see them. I always said that these things were pointless. What would you get from seeing the sunrise and the sunset? I used to say what is the point of climbing a mountain when you will be down again? What is the point of seeing the sea? It's just a massive spot of water. Actually, that's what I told my students when I gave lessons. Also, I said that to the main journalist when I worked as a translator in a part-time job. I also said to a lot of people that life is in black and white in my eyes."

"Tell me about all the places that you want to see, and I will help you go there," Arkon said.

"You need money for that!" Then she said wryly, "You needed to bring something magical from Meridian that can make wishes come true. Also, we both are without jobs, so how shall we do that?" Arkon stared at her with one eye. Then he went to his room to make a call.

He called Cornelia, but when she first picked up, she yelled, "Don't call me ever." When he spoke, she hung up.

Meanwhile, Tynar visited Nani in her shop, and she launched into a confusing line of questions involving Arya and wet shoes. She thought she had another dream, and she blinked up at Tynar when he said it was not, explaining that he and Arkon had come back. He took Nani with him, so Arkon was annoyed when Tynar brought Nani to the house, banishing Tynar from his presence. And Arya told Nani bashfully that Arkon returned because he missed her.

Tynar followed Arkon upstairs and explained that he only went to Nani to ask for work. She'd given him a job sitting at her shop, saying that he inspired her and stabilized her abilities since her mystical powers come and go. He laughed that she's just like Arkon, who scowled at him darkly, then realized that they needed the money. "Okay, do your best at this job."

Downstairs, Arya explained that Arkon came back to say goodbye properly. Nani sobbed that Arya made her feel sorry because she was a millionaire's daughter and didn't have to worry about money. She admitted that it doesn't happen very often, but she felt bad and really wants Arya to be happy.

Arkon came down and found the girls wailing and hugging, and he thought to himself that they were weird and kept walking. He called Arya later to tell her he was going to see Cornelia. But Arya kept asking over and over why he was going there, and Arkon evaded her questions and asked if she was jealous. Arya swore that she was cool with him having immortal female friends, and Arkon told her that he got very jealous of human male friends! So Arya added, "Well, I can be a little jealous sometimes!" Then she told Arkon that she was going to work a part-time job today. She said it was for a human male friend, then she hung up, giving Arkon a taste of his own medicine.

Immediately after, she received a frantic call from Matt and rushed to her office, where she learned that Chairman Hale had sold the building. Luckily, the new landlord said they could stay and even lowered the deposit and monthly rent. She didn't know that the new owner was Julian.

After her part-time sessions at the resort, Julian told Arya that his employees love coming to her for stress relief. She told him that a miracle happened and she wouldn't lose her clinic, and Julian congratulated her and asked if she was free for dinner, though he already knew she was going to decline. He said that he knew she wouldn't be free for dinner for a long time and told her that he'd wait!

He walked her out, musing that the new owner of her building was probably a warm and generous man who was also probably very classy and handsome! Arya has hair stuck in her eyelashes, so Julian grabbed her hand to stop her from messing with it and then gently brushed the hair out of her face. Caleb, who had come to see Cornelia's filming here, stopped when he saw that, and he marched over to them angrily. When Arya saw him approaching, she asked loudly, "What are you doing here?"

Caleb stared angrily at Julian and said, "I can't see you spending time with our servant!"

Then he turned on Arya. "I'm distraught to see you spending time with him, and you know who he really is." Arya was confused because she didn't know what he was talking about. He accused Arya of keeping Julian in reserve for after Arkon leaves. Then he grabbed her by the arm. Juliane snatched Caleb's hand away, and in the scuffle, Caleb knocked Arya to the ground. When she looked up, both Caleb and Julian were gone!

Caleb transported Julian to a secluded location, where he proposed that they just fight and get it over with. Julian refused to fight without reason, not accepting that Caleb just hated his very existence. Looking a bit unhinged, Caleb said he just doesn't like that an abnormal being like Julian exists, but Julian decided he could live with that and turned to go.

Caleb continued taunting Julian, insisting that he'd make him pay for his past sins. Julian yelled that he hadn't committed any sins, so Caleb threw the first punch. He snarled that his reason was the fact that Julian didn't know his sin, so he punched him again. But Caleb said that his biggest reason, the one that made him crazy, was that he hated himself because of Julian! Julian hit Caleb, knocking him to the ground. Caleb realized that Menar was nearby and warned him not to interfere, so Menar called Cornelia instead. Cornelia was refusing to give Arkon a single penny, not even when he made it a royal order and threatened to punish her. At the same time, Arkon got a call from Arya, who was frantic that Caleb had taken Julian somewhere.

Julian and Caleb continued fighting, and Caleb joked that it was not like they could kill each other. Julian corrected him, reminding Caleb that he *can* kill. In response, Caleb charged up his powers and smashed Julian with a force wave.

Provoked, Julian stood up, then hurled a ball of his black power at Caleb. But at the last second, Menar threw himself in front of Caleb, taking the death blow meant for his friend. Caleb yelled at Menar for interfering, and Julian looked horrified at what he had done. Julian looked down at Menar's scorched face, which triggered a memory—bodies lying dead in a cave, one of them with Menar's face! His twin? Julian even remembered that Caleb was there then. He screamed with grief.

Caleb saw Julian's stunned reaction and asked if he remembered whom he killed now. Julian stood there shaking, and nearby, Cornelia and Arkon shaped from the air and appeared there.

Being left behind at the hotel, Arya recalled what Caleb said about her knowing who Julian really was. She started putting the clues together, between the vague things that Arkon had said and the time she saw Julian's instantly healing wound. She finally realized and said, "Oh my God. I thought I was wrong."

At the fighting place. "What happened here?" Cornelia asked with shock. She repeated, "What is happening? What do you mean? Who was killed?"

She looked at Julian while he was terrified, and Arkon was just staring, not realizing what was happening. Cornelia remembered Menar's words, 'because of me', then she turned to Caleb and asked, "Did he kill Menar's twin?"

Caleb replied, "Yes, and now Menar's turn came." Then he shook Menar, but he was unconscious. Caleb looked with anger at Julian, then he stood and said, "For 2850 years, I imagined how to kill you thousands of times since you killed everybody in that cave to protect the traitorous woman that betrayed Arkon! But I was satisfied that you were locked in that cave to live your life circle and die, reborn and die there. I didn't know that you escaped, but you lived and made a life here under the sunlight. How could you!"

He grabbed his jacket to punch him; then Arkon said calmly, "Enough." He approached them and held Caleb's hand down. He put his hand down and walked two steps; then he instantly teleported to another place. Arkon stared at Julian; then he took Menar and Cornelia to Caleb's place.

Cornelia said, "Caleb is not answering my calls! I didn't understand what he said. When did he meet him for the first time? And what is that cave that he talked about?"

Arkon asked, "Do you think that Menar will be fine? And who is Menar's twin?"

Cornelia replied, "Yes, I think so because Julian didn't use his full power. He can be healed, but he will stay asleep for a while. Don't you remember him? He was in Meridian. He was Caleb's shadow. He loved him very much. It was Menar's twin. I also didn't know what happened. I realized recently that I hadn't seen that servant a long time ago."

"Why did he kill him?" Arkon asked.

"I don't know, but I was shocked by Mr. Julian," Cornelia replied.

Meanwhile, Julian was still in a state of shock, his ugly past having been brought to the forefront of his mind by his actions today. He was haunted by Caleb's words that he didn't deserve freedom, and he huddled alone in an abandoned building, shaking and crying.

Arya was back home when Arkon returned. She asked him, "He is one of you, right?" She could see the answer on his face. "I mean Julian. Is he from the world of Meridian?" He hesitated, and Arya added, "Why didn't you tell me?"

"Why? Why are you asking about him? You didn't ask me before either. He is not one of us!" Arkon replied.

"But…" Arya uttered, then realized something. She stared into Arkon's eyes and said, "It must be one of you who told Julian he shouldn't even be born!"

"When? When did you have this kind of conversation? Are you close enough to talk about these things?" Arkon barked.

But Arya asked, "Why did you tell him this kind of thing? You are a higher creature. Why did you behave like humans?"

He asked jealously if they started talking after he left, or even earlier. Then something in his voice turned vulnerable as he asked Arya if she was hoping he would leave! He got angry again and asked if she broke down in tears after he left instead of enduring and if she gave her heart away so easily because of that. Arya gaped incredulously as Arkon darkly reminded her that he is a very jealous and irrational immortal. He left her and went upstairs. He sat alone and remembered a conversation he once had with Caleb in the realm of Meridian.

FLASHBACK – MERIDIAN

Arkon stood at Vision Lake, and Caleb was next to him. He asked Caleb, "I heard that Tylen hid in a cave in Loraoza (a place in Meridian)."

"No matter where she is, she will not be safe anywhere because we will find her," Caleb replied.

"I didn't mean that I wanted to protect her. I will not forgive her, but I want to ask her what I meant for her. That is all."

END FLASHBACK

"This is impossible," Arkon said. Arkon started to think that the cave he sent Caleb to find Tylen was the same cave that Julian was kept in, but he couldn't understand why Caleb hid that from him.

The next morning, Arya called Nani for advice, asking 'for a friend' why someone would suddenly get angry in the middle of a conversation. Nani barked, "Break up with him!" Arya shot down Nani's guess that the guy has anger issues or is a jerk, but Nani nailed it when she said that he probably feels guilty about something! And that's why he changed his tone last time.

Meanwhile, Arkon went to meet Caleb on top of a skyscraper, overlooking the city. When Arkon approached him, he said, "Tell me, did you go to that cave 2850 years ago? Did you meet him there? Is that the same cave where Menar's twin died? You said that you would not help me on that day, so why did you go there?"

Caleb exploded with anger. "Yes, I want there, but I regret it thousands of times. Why did I give you that favor, why!"

Arkon asked, "What happened that day? What was Julian doing there?"

"He was trapped there, and she was also hiding there in the same cave when my friend and I arrived there; we saw a child with her. I didn't know who he was, but he thought that we wanted to take Tylen. Meanwhile, the guards of the queen arrived. They wanted to take her, so that creature killed everyone there with his dark power," Caleb replied.

Arkon's eyes filled with tears, and he yelled, "Why? Why did you hide that from me for thousands of years?"

A voice from behind said loudly, "This was the order of the king!" They turned to find Menar and Cornelia.

Then Menar continued, "The king ordered us not to tell anyone about that child who we saw in the cave, and we were forced to obey the king's orders."

Arkon said in grief, "Then he died because of me."

But Menar said, "I'm sorry, Your Highness, but my brother's death was no one's responsibility, as you know when twin immortal servants are born, one of them must die someday, and that was my brother's destiny."

But Cornelia approached Arkon and said, "That *was* his fault." Then she punched him in the face!

She took Caleb's hand and led him away. Cornelia took Caleb home and said that she knew he's carrying around a lot of hatred and anger, especially for himself, and she asked him to let it go. She said that she knew he felt guilty for running away as if he had abandoned Menar's twin, but he just scowled at her and turned to walk away.

She called after him, "I'm sorry." He turned to her, then she continued, "I'm the one who must feel sorry; don't you think that? I told you to run away if you see him when we were in Meridian." She took two steps toward him. "Are these words provoking you?"

"No," Caleb replied. "Then why did you run away? Menar told me that he forced you to get you out that day; don't blame yourself," Cornelia replied.

"You know nothing."

"No, I know what you were thinking. Part of you was blessed because Menar took you out of the cave that day, and the other part was in grief because you left your friend's killer," Cornelia replied. And she approached him closely. She put her hand on his chest, then said, "You didn't leave your friend, but you saved the other, and if something had happened to you that day, then Menar would not exist today." She caught his face with her hands and kissed him softly on the lips. "This is the greatest comfort I can give you," Cornelia said.

She pulled back and asked if he was all better now, and Caleb scoffed, "Are you kidding me?" And pulled her closer to kiss her again.

In the meantime, Julian was still huddled in the abandoned building when the little blind girl came looking for him. She said that she could feel he was there, but Julian didn't respond to her, not even when she tripped and fell, though it nearly killed him not to help her. Eventually, the little girl left, and as soon as she was gone, Julian's anger and self-hatred exploded. He screamed and threw things until he ran out of steam, then bowed to his knees and sobbed.

In Arya's room in her house, she sat on her bed, thinking about Julian. Arya tried to figure out what Arkon meant when he said that Julian wasn't one of them. She remembered Julian saying that he didn't know his mother, and his father treated him like a monster and kept him locked up so others wouldn't find out about him.

She also recalled that Arkon once said that the concept of family is very different in the realm of the immortals. Something occurred to her, and she asked herself what she planned to do when she saw Julian again. She changed her clothes and went downstairs. Looking into the wall mirror, she thought, *I forget that I have all this beauty on my face.* The house door opened, and Arkon entered and saw her standing there. "Are you going out?" Arkon asked.

"No," Arya replied. Arkon immediately approached her and hugged her.

"I'm sorry about yesterday."

"Did something happen?" Arya asked.

Arkon shook his head, saying, "No." She smiled.

"Okay then, forget it. Where have you been all day? Did you try to borrow some money from your friends?" Arkon smiled lightly and nodded. Arya continued, "It sounds like they rejected your request. Welcome to reality, Your Highness, but don't worry, I will make you forget. I will make you a fine dinner, but I need to go to the grocery shop, so you should peel the potatoes, and I'd back soon with the other ingredients." She got out and headed to the grocery store.

Meanwhile, he saw a cute picture of Arya on a beach, and he decided to take it out of the frame to straighten it. The whole thing fell apart, and when he picked it up, he saw another photo behind the first. It was a picture of Arya as a child with her father. This was the first time he saw Arya's father. Arkon put the pictures back as he had found them. On her way home, Arya was distracted looking up Italian recipes on her phone. Suddenly, someone grabbed her from behind, and when Arkon went outside to meet her, all he found were the groceries and Arya's phone lying on the ground.

In the car, it was Herbert who took Arya, but she was still screaming bloody murder, and she tried to escape once he stopped the car. He grabbed her and yelled that he just wanted her to see Julian, so she stopped fighting. She found Julian in the abandoned building, still curled up in a ball of misery. He tried to leave when he saw her; he yelled at her to go, but she grabbed him in a back hug and ordered him to be still. She said soothingly that it was okay, and Julian heaved a big sigh and relaxed.

Meanwhile, in Caleb's penthouse, Arkon, Cornelia, and Caleb were there, calling Arya's phone, but she didn't answer. One of Arkon's calls worked, and Arya finally picked up. "Where are you?" Arkon asked.

"Don't worry, I'm fine," Arya replied. "Is that jerk the reason? Tell me your location, or come back home now," Arkon replied.

"There is no need to worry. I'm fine. I will come soon."

"Come back home. You don't know him. He's not as you think," Arkon insisted.

"I know enough! Don't worry. I will be back soon." Then she ended the call. Arkon was very mad at her at that moment.

Cornelia said, "I told you she was fine with Julian! You thought he was going to hurt her, but it's the opposite. Maybe Julian is dangerous, but he will not hurt her. Maybe she is on his farm. Let him have her. That's better for her anyway!"

Arkon stared at her angrily and said, "Help me to get there instantly."

"No, I will not help you!" Cornelia responded. Then she added, "Think about her; Julian can help her. She's a human; money is what all she needs, and Julian can give her what she wants!"

Arya went back to where Julian was sitting on the bare ground; she approached him, and he was looking at the ground. Arya said, "Mr. Julian." But Julian told her to leave, then she repeated, "Julian."

But Julian yelled, "Please leave; don't be close to me. I destroy everything. If you stay with me, you will be miserable! I almost killed you once. Some things cannot be changed." He started to shake, and the tears poured out. "However, I tried. I couldn't change. I always go back to the past. I always go back repeatedly."

"You say that your sins cannot be forgiven," Arya said.

"Yes, I can commit other sins anytime because I will not change," Julian replied.

"No, you are wrong. You are not this kind of human."

Julian said wryly, "Human?"

Arya replied, "Yes, human, because I don't think you want to be called an immortal! What do you prefer, to be human or an immortal?" She got Julian's attention, then she continued, "Being human describes you better. You helped a lot of people. You supported a lot of children. Also, you helped a lot of sick people get better. You saved a lot of people's lives in many different ways. Do you know what you mean for those whom you helped? You are like a god for them. The work that you did as a human was God's work. Let's say that God is looking at you now from the sky. What would he see? He will see a simple man who is trying to help others as much as he can in a small country on this planet called Earth. Julian, you are blessed…"

His tears stopped, and he looked into Arya's eyes. Then Arya said, "All the trees that you planted here will be a forest someday soon, and all the good you did made you more than a human. Don't doubt me because I've never seen a human like you. If you choose to be a human, I will be beside you forever. I will be your close friend."

A voice came from behind, calling 'Arya'. She turned and saw Arkon standing at the door. He approached her and caught her hands tightly. Then he glanced at Julian's eyes angrily and pulled Arya out of the place to leave.

In the car, silence took hold, but Arya said, "I'm his therapist. I can't let him be in pain and do nothing. Are you jealous?" He spoke no word; then he caught her hand and glanced straight. When they arrived home, Arya asked him if he had eaten while she was there. Arya offered to make him something to eat. Instead, he whirled her around and kissed her hard, and though she was confused, Arya kissed him back. Arkon walked her back up the stairs and pushed her onto the couch, never breaking the kiss, but just as things were getting hot and heavy, he suddenly jumped up with his hands in the air. Somehow in total control, he said they should stop, and Arya blurted out, "Why?" Arkon stuck his nose in the air and said that candy shouldn't be eaten all at once! Then he wished Arya a good night and went to his roof room.

In the morning, he did frantic push-ups to work off his excess energy as Arya sat on the couch, twitching and trying to chase the thoughts of that searing kiss out of her mind. Meanwhile, she received a message from Julian:

'Good morning, Arya. Can we meet for a little time?'

When Arya arrived at Julian's office, she found him with the little blind girl, drawing pictures of the flowers they planted. Arya realized the girl was blind, but she didn't say anything about it, and the little girl precociously asked if this is Arya that she overheard Julian talking to regarding a promise that had to be kept.

The girl said that he was in a really good mood at the time, and Julian looked so embarrassed. He tried to interject awkwardly, and then he was saved by Secretary Nigel's return.

After sending the girl home, Julian explained to Arya that the little girl was his neighbor and his only friend, and that her blindness was his fault. He explained that he struggled to control his powers for the first few years he was in the human world. He told Arya that on his first day at his farm, the little girl's grandmother left the infant girl alone for a few moments, and a wild dog attacked her. In his haste, he'd used his power to get the dog off of the girl, and his power had killed the dog and damaged the girl's eyes. He said that now he feels responsible for the girl and lives his life as if it were hers. When Arya didn't respond, he told her that he'd just decided something—that it's not a bad idea to enjoy this regardless of her intentions.

Arya was confused, but Julian just smiled and said she didn't need to know what he meant. He said that he feels like they've met before, a long time ago, remembering her soothing words when she'd given him a back hug. He'd heard those exact words being said once before, but in a man's voice!

In the meantime, at Nani's booth, Tynar responded to a summons from Nani and found her asleep in her shop. She talked in her sleep, and Tynar adorably answered her; then he leaped back in a fighting stance when she suddenly cried out. She was dreaming about Arya again, the same dream, unable to hear what Arya was saying to her. In the dream, Arya looked towards the door, saying, "That person…that person is the one who saved me, but…" and then her voice faded again. They both saw someone walking into the room, shoes soaking wet, but she still doesn't see the other person's face.

Nani jerked awake with a shriek, startling poor Tynar all over again. She said that she was dreaming about Arya bragging about her boyfriend saving her life. Then she perked up and decided that Tynar must really be good for her powers because having him there enabled her to hear Arya in the dream. Finally, she thought that the man in the dream was Arya's boyfriend.

Arya came back to her clinic and cleaned the office in anticipation of the building's new owner coming to visit; she didn't know yet that Julian was the new owner because he wanted to surprise her, but Matt got a call from a sick friend and had to leave. Arya knew that Arkon was on his way to pick her up. Arya picked up her phone to call him, and she was startled when she imagined him posing on the screen. She shook it off and face-timed Arkon, choosing an app that added little kitten ears and whiskers to her face. Arkon's reaction was funny, but not as funny as Arya's when his image morphed into a picture of what happened between them yesterday. She screamed, and Arkon screamed back, and Arya quickly hung up.

Arkon headed downstairs to leave and found Caleb standing in Arya's living room. "What are you doing here?" Arkon asked.

Caleb smiled wryly and said, "Staying here made you forget who you are, and you forgot that we can appear wherever we want." Then Caleb grumpily said that Cornelia made him come and listen to Arkon, and Arkon said again that Menar's brother died because of him and that he's lived all this time without even knowing it. He apologized to Caleb, adding that Julian was probably trying to protect Tylen that day. Caleb said that he needs time to process that.

Arya was about to jump out of her skin as she was waiting for Arkon, so she went to get drinks for the building owner. Arkon arrived before she returned, and he was not pleased to find Julian waiting in Arya's office. Julian said that he was here as the new landlord. Then, when Arkon didn't know what that meant, Julian smirked that it was someone who was sometimes more powerful than a king! Arkon told Julian to leave, but Julian just reminded Arkon that he'd still be here with Arya when Arkon returned to the realm of the immortals.

When Arkon was about to punch Julian, Arya opened the office room, entered, and approached them. She stared at Julian and asked, "Mr. Julian, I don't think that we have an appointment today!"

"I thought you would know that I'd come today," Julian replied.

Arya was confused, and she said, "You didn't say that you would come when I saw you today—"

Arkon interrupted her, saying, "Don't say anything! Don't talk to him." He got the office keys from the table, threw them at Julian, and said, "Close the door when you leave and put the keys in the rose pot."

Then he took Arya's hand and left the clinic.

Arkon drove like a bat out of hell as Arya smiled at his obvious display of jealousy. She chirped that he was charming even when he was jealous, earning an incredulous look from Arkon and completely defusing his anger. They decided to go see the sunset, and they ended up on a rock outcropping overlooking the sea. As the sun went down, Arya told Arkon that she had come here once with her parents, but they argued so much that it just made her anxious.

She saw that Arkon was amused, so she asked him, "What are you thinking about?"

He sighed and said, "Tomorrow, the day after tomorrow, and the day after that. A day when I'm no longer here with you."

Arya told him to only think of today and reminded him that he once told her about people who are able to live the rest of their lives with the memories of today.

Darkness fell, and Arya mused that when something fades in the sun, it becomes history, and if it is bathed in the moonlight, it becomes a myth, and the people will talk about the story of a great immortal king who came from his world and loved a human girl. She said that their story would become a myth, and Arkon leaned over and kissed her for a very long time. He felt and heard three beats, like a heartbeat. He turned left and right, and his facial expressions changed. Arya asked, "What's wrong?"

He looked at her and said, "The jewel; I feel the jewel! The Great Jewel of Meridian is near…"

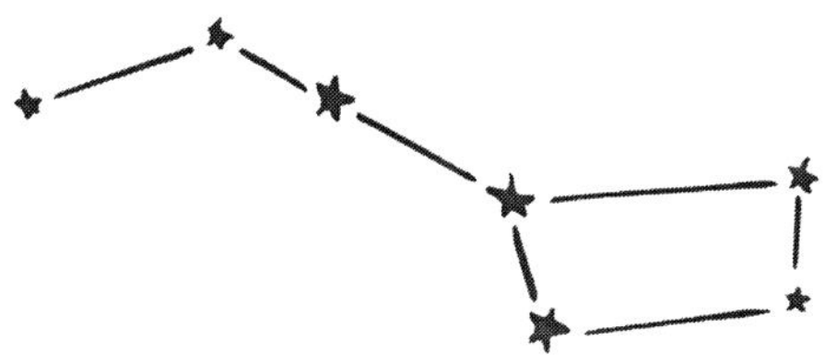

Chapter Ten
I Will Find Him

In Meridian, Queen Wera sat on the edge of the Visions Lake as usual. "Time is growing short for the prince and Arya, who struggle to face their eventual separation in very different ways. One broods while the other chooses denial, and neither option seems very desirable. They're trying to make the best of the time they have left, but there are still a few mysteries to solve before Arkon leaves for good this time," the queen stated.

A veiled woman approached the queen and said, "You're admiring watching them, my lady!" The queen turned and smiled.

"It's been a very long time, Halinor!" The queen stood and hugged Halinor.

Then Halinor took two steps from the lake and said, "You gave birth to a real prince, my lady, but it seems that his heart is controlling him. When I saw him, I knew that he was the one in the prophecy. Doesn't that bother you?"

The queen replied, "No, I'm ready for that moment when it will come because I too want to help the realm of humans. Also, his decision is not clear because he hasn't found the jewel yet because he is still resisting his heart, but you gave both of them your help with your advice. I didn't expect that you would be interfering that much."

"I also didn't expect that, but this girl came through much pain, and I wanted to help. It's sad that she must come through the pain one last time," Halinor replied.

On earth, Arkon remained looking for the jewel, but there was no place to look because it was only a sand beach and water. Arya said, "Come on. There is nothing to look for here." Arkon came back and sat next to her in the car as they sat there watching the stars. Arya laughed at herself, explaining that even though it's a very romantic atmosphere, she keeps thinking about pizza.

Suddenly, she asked Arkon, "What do you think about my father? Why did he leave alone and didn't come back even after my mother's death?" This reminded Arkon of Arya's impassioned demand that he find her father, and he asked if she'd tried looking for him. She said she didn't because she feared discovering that he had been in the same country all this time and never came for her. Arkon asked if her wish was still to see her father and say what she needed to say, but Arya just said uncertainly, "I think so."

On their way back home, Arya kept staring at Arkon, and his hand was holding hers. She didn't want that moment to come to an end. She felt safe and comfortable. When they approached Arya's home, she asked, "Do you know why people get married here? Because they don't want to separate after they spend a beautiful day together, but we already live together, and we don't have to separate; it's really lovely to live together under the same roof." When they arrived home and sat to drink coffee, Arya asked, "How is the relation between you and your mother, Queen Wera?"

Arkon was shocked, and his facial expression changed. "How did you know the queen's name?" he asked.

"Well, come with me."

They went upstairs, and Arya took out the book that she took from the library months ago and put it on the table in front of Arkon's eyes and said, "I know it's hard to believe, but I found this book in a giant library, and the librarian gave it to me."

Arkon took the book immediately, and he was in great shock. He said, "This is a history book about the great world of Meridian, but how did it come here?" She explained to him that she read everything in this book, and that helped her understand the world of Meridian.

She asked him to sit on the couch to watch a movie together. Arya sat primly across the couch, but Arkon patted his knee and insisted that she lay her head in his lap, and she did, asking what made him think of this, and he said he read her diary and saw this in a poem she wrote as a child. It pretty much went, 'Daddy's lap is mine. Go away, Matt!' over and over. After giving Arkon a quick glare, Arya settled in and found a cooking show. She commented that he should cook for the rest of the time he was here, but the mention of Arkon leaving has them both silent. Arya asked when he'd leave, so Arkon said, "No idea. If I fail to find the jewel, I will be trapped in Meridian for more than a thousand years and retake the mission again."

Arya pondered that their relationship has a time limit, comparing it to terminal patients she met when she was an intern. She told Arkon that she didn't know how they felt when they completed their treatment, but now she knew how to prepare for goodbyes and what happened afterward!

"Can I ask you something? How do you deal with this? I have 40 or 50 years to live, but your life is eternity! Can I be greedy? Can I ask you to remember me as much as you can?" Drops of tears started pouring from her eyes. Arkon just sighed, then leaned down and kissed her cheek.

The next morning, Arya woke up on the living room floor, where it was obvious they had both spent the night. To smell delicious smells coming from the kitchen, she walked to the kitchen to find the most handsome chef ever, making various types of food. She smiled happily and asked, "What are you doing?"

Arkon turned to her and said, "Did you wake up! I just woke up early, and I had nothing to do. That's why I decided to cook something special."

Arya smiled and said wryly, "Oh, that's right, and what after that? Are you making me a special meal because I asked you yesterday?"

Arkon immediately answered, "No, that is only because I'm hungry."

"Oh, okay, then I will go back to sleep! However, I'm not used to having breakfast, especially in the morning."

Arkon stopped chopping and said strictly, "Sit down."

"Okay, then I can't say no, and you insist, so I will go wash and come back fast," Arya replied. She went to the bathroom to brush her teeth, thinking it was a shame that he'd only get angry if she told him how cute he was. She got back to the table to find Arkon laying out a huge feast, and she felt overwhelmed, having never had anyone cook for her before.

They sat to eat, and Arkon said, "Please start."

Arya replied, "So, this is the feeling when someone cooks for you." He put the spoon in her hand and stared into her eyes. Meanwhile, the doorbell rang.

It was Julian returning the office keys. Arya invited him in. He and Arkon glowered at each other. Then Arkon inexplicably invited Julian to join them for breakfast. Arya was alarmed, especially when Arkon started insulting her cooking and listing her bad qualities to Julian. Arya cut them and said, "Please, Mr. Julian, would you like a cup of tea?"

Arkon replied angrily, "No, it's not the time for tea!"

Julian replied, "There is nothing like that. We can drink tea anytime."

"I have this rule in my house. We don't drink tea in the morning!" Arkon replied. He sat and continued, "We have breakfast at this time, so if you don't want to eat, just leave."

"Okay, then I will have breakfast with you!" Julian said. Arya opened her eyes widely and sighed. Julian sat in front of Arkon and said, "Miss Arya, you cook delicious and beautiful meals."

"She didn't cook that! I did everything myself," Arkon stated. And Arya freaked out. Arkon said pointedly that he always has to carry Arya to bed, trying to make Julian jealous. He added that he took a bath every morning, but it made Arya shy to see him naked! Hilariously, he made the innocent truth sound dirty. Unruffled, Julian managed to shock Arya even further by informing her that he was the new owner of her office building. She was thrilled, and Arkon grew jealous at the mention of Julian's money.

"I told you I would buy the whole building because I have a lot of money!" Julian replied while he was staring at Arkon.

Arya was very happy to hear that; she said, "Oh, my god, I'm really grateful, Mr. Julian." Arkon was shocked, staring at her with an exclamation mark.

Julian replied, "No, please, you don't have to be grateful because I did that with all the tenants in the building because the rent was very high."

"Even so, you did a great thing; thank you," Arya replied.

Then suddenly, Arkon yelled, "I'm a king." He put his nose in the air and repeated, "I'm a king!" But Julian smiled wryly, raised his eyebrows, and finished his plate.

After breakfast, Julian looked around and found a photo of Arya and Nani from college. He remembered Arya's back hug and the familiar words she said, and he asked again if they'd never met before. And she replied, "I don't think so, because if I had met you before, I would remember you."

Arkon ordered Julian to sit and Arya to make tea, and she sighed at the sight of the Meridian king and a half-immortal sitting in her living room. Arkon demanded his tea in his coffee mug, imperiously informing Julian that he has his own mug, which depicts the harmonious relationship between master and servant! Arkon asked Julian, "Why are you really here?" Julian said that you could make an opponent reveal his shortcomings if you poke him. He reminded Arkon that he was good at waiting, but Arkon quipped that he'd waste his life waiting needlessly.

On his way out, Julian reminded Arya that she was due to work on his farm in two days. Arkon refused to allow it, but Julian said it would pay him back for breaking the land sale contract. Julian said, "See you later, Arya." Then he left the house.

Arya looked at Arkon and said, "This is because you prevented me from selling the land." Arkon stared angrily and stormed upstairs.

Arkon called and asked Cornelia for money again to pay off Arya's debt to Julian, but she just hung on to him. She told Caleb smugly that Julian was doing exactly as she instructed, but Caleb grimaced at the sound of that name. He brought Cornelia breakfast in bed, telling her that it's a fantasy for human women to get the man they love to do this. She quipped, "Shouldn't it be with a man I love, though?" Caleb asked how much more he has to do, but she just said, "Go out. I want to shower." Outside her room, Caleb sighed, saying that she was the most difficult woman in the world. But then he smiled and said he knew that already. He got a call from Arkon and turned down his request to meet today, and on his end, Arkon threatened that once he gets his powers back, he will take their powers for a thousand years.

Arkon didn't have anyone else, so he called his loyal servant Tynar, who was at his job. "Are you earning a lot of money?"

Tynar hesitated and replied, "Yes, I am. It's good you called me, Your Highness. Van called me and told me to inform you that you should stay and wait for him because he said that he has something important to tell you about."

"Why did he call you instead of calling me directly?" Arkon asked.

"Because Lady Cornelia told him not to call you because she told him that you are always looking for money!" Tynar replied.

Again at Nani's Booth, Nani was still trying to interpret her dream involving Arya and how she heard Arya saying, "That person saved me. But." But everything after that was inaudible, and again Arya turned to look at someone, but all Nani could see was a pair of wet shoes. Meanwhile, when Tynar arrived at work, Nani started to ask for his advice. But she got distracted and lost her train of thought. She called Arya and asked, "Are you okay?"

"Oh, I think you want me to be in trouble!" Arya replied.

"My friend, you became sassy after a hard relationship," Nani said.

"No, my relationship wasn't bad," Arya replied. And Nani insisted, "Then, are you thrilled because you are letting your man go?"

Arya corrected her that they do not love to break up but if they have to they like to break up properly. Nani replied, "My friend, you are awful." Arya hung up.

Meanwhile, in the restaurant, Caleb finally came to meet Arkon after his insistence. When he entered, he saw Arkon shining like usual, wearing a neat white suit. He approached and commented, "You are shining, and all the girls here, even men, are looking at you. I always forget how you are the most handsome creature in Meridian and even here."

Arkon smiled and replied, "This is a great compliment from you—"

Caleb interrupted him, saying, "Don't think that means that I'll give you what you want." He sat in front of him.

Arkon said, "If you pay me now, I will give you what you want when I go back to Meridian."

Caleb replied, "Does that mean you will not search for the jewel! I knew that you came back to see Arya, but I couldn't believe that you would waste your time and leave the jewel for a thousand years more!"

"Don't change the subject. This is not your business. I called because I want to know what you want instead of giving me money," Arkon replied.

"I can give you everything you want—money and diamond—but Cornelia wouldn't be accepted, and I will not bother my woman because of you," Caleb replied.

"In this world on the internet, the humans call people like you weak!" Arkon said.

"Well, I don't mind that," Caleb replied.

"I'm leaving," Arkon said. But Caleb stopped him.

"Wait, I need you!"

Arkon was astonished. "What's wrong?"

Caleb asked hesitantly, "Cornelia…how can I get Cornelia's heart?"

Arkon smiled a creepy smile and said, "Well, you know that Cornelia is the most loyal among us, but when she leaves someone, she never comes back for him."

Caleb asked, "How do you keep your relation stable with her even after all these years and even when you knew that she loved you?"

"I thought you realized that I'm an exception in Cornelia's life!" Arkon replied.

Caleb's facial expressions changed, and he said, "I thought you were really suitable to ask you; you don't know her well."

He wanted to stand, but Arkon said, "You are an idiot. Cornelia didn't love me as you thought; she always cared about you, but she didn't show that!" Caleb was shocked by that, but he didn't give Arkon what he wanted.

Arkon stomped home, fuming, having been refused yet again. He ran into Arya on her way to Julian's farm, so he barked that he forbade her to go. They both ended up on Julian's farm digging holes in the ground. Arya apologized to Julian because Arkon insisted on coming with her, but Julian was actually impressed with how hard Arkon was working. Arya warned Julian that Arkon thinks his day's work is worth about fifty billion dollars because he's a prince and the next king of Meridian, and she told him that he expected to be paid minus the land sale cancellation fees! Julian joined Arkon and told him that his idea was good, but the execution was clumsy. He asked if Arkon believed that money was all Arya would want him for, and Arkon retorted that Julian knew nothing about Arya and hadn't gotten a chance with her.

Julian informed Arkon that as an immortal there's something he doesn't know about Arya. "Humans are lonely from the moment they're born; she doesn't need the money, and she doesn't want anything else except your existence beside her, and that will not be possible in your case!"

Heading off to plant a tree, Julian told Arya to join Arkon. She asked if Arkon was really that big of a deal in the realm of Meridian, so Julian revealed, "I spent my life there trapped in a cave, so I don't know a lot about the other immortals or details about that place, but based on all the stories that Herbert told me about the immortals, Arkon was always at the center of them. He is able to do anything, and he was born to be the next king of that world." But he added that there were two things Arkon couldn't do—he can't revive the dead, and he doesn't have Julian's power.

"Are you okay? He may leave tomorrow. Maybe you will wake up the next morning, and you will not find him then!" Julian asked.

"He came back to say goodbye properly and to find his jewel, and then he will leave. I understand that, and I'm not waiting for something else," Arya replied. She left Julian and went to give Arkon a cup of cold water. When she approached him, she stopped there beside the tree, looking at him while he was working. She didn't know how she would be able to let him go soon, but she cut her thoughts off and walked to him to give him water. He took the glass and poured it on himself. It was hilarious how Arya completely ignored Arkon's attempt at seduction, instead just laughing at him, she got a towel to dry his hair. He submitted like a good puppy, frowning when she said that her heart was just fine after his performance. Then he let her lead him to a chair.

He was genuinely disappointed at Arya's reaction to seeing him all wet, and he asked why she didn't react like she did the first time she saw him bathing. Sadly, he said that if she only has forty or fifty years to live, she should have more memories of him so that she never runs out!

"How can you say that? You are very brilliant saying these things like they're not important. You make me feel that you have the heart of a rock," Arya said.

He looked into her eyes and said, "I don't say that because I don't care." He grabbed her waist and hugged her, then said, "You know that I'm selfish, right? So I'm doing that because I'm selfish. I'm asking you now to do your hard work and don't be alone ever!"

Arya put her hand on his shoulder and said, "I will remember you for a really long time." From a not-so-far spot, Julian watched them, and he realized that Arya was not for him, no matter how hard he would try.

On their way back home, Arya asked, "Are you angry because he didn't pay you what you wanted?" She added that the offer that Julian did make was very generous. She thought that they should go back every day and work. She took Arkon's hand, saying, "Let's stay together until the last moment you have here." They kept walking until they arrived at Arya's house gate. They saw a woman in a red dress. When the woman turned, they realized that it was Cornelia.

She asked, "Where have you been?" She stared at him and saw his dirty clothes. "What were you doing?"

But Arkon replied, "What are you doing here?"

She smiled and said, "I carry happy news for me! Congratulations! The time has come; you have only a few days here. The gate opened. You know that means you have only a really short time on earth. I still can't believe that you wasted all your time and wasted valuable days messing with this human girl and didn't search for the jewel. I can't believe that you postponed your inauguration for more thousand years." Arya's heart squeezed from the inside, and Cornelia walked two steps and turned.

"I will say that in case you think to do that, you know what would happen if you did not come back at the right time, right? Especially without the jewel…" Then she walked away and disappeared.

Arya stared into Arkon's eyes, and they were filled with tears. Then she smiled and said, "Let's go inside. I'm hungry." She made a simple meal, and they sat, but Arkon just picked at his food. Arya said that it was not like he had to leave immediately, but Arkon looked at her with the saddest eyes. He asked why she never asks him not to leave, even if she doesn't mean it.

Arya asked him if he would stay, and he said wearily, "No. I can't do that." So Arya said cheerfully that she's not a woman who holds men back in life, but Arkon just kept staring at her sadly. She said that she's not stopping him because if he weren't the prince of the great world of Meridian, he wouldn't be nearly as cool as he is. She told him that he's just an unemployed bum who likes taking baths and driving cars. With every word, the light went out of his eyes until finally he got up and walked away.

As he walked away, Arya sighed, saying that he's much too sensitive to be a king. But once she was alone, she couldn't hold back her tears any longer, and she went to her room and sat on the window ledge, looking at the moonlight. She spent the night crying alone.

The next morning, Cornelia woke up, and a grin was on her face. Caleb noticed that and asked, "Are you happy that much?"

"You should have seen the glare on his face when I told him yesterday. I thought the sky would fall," Cornelia replied.

"He must be bothered by you very much!" Caleb said.

"I thought I would not tell him about the gate sign."

"That's really callous of you. You know that if he stays here without the jewel, he will die! Can you live without him? He will be forced to come back, so leave him to his problems; don't make it worse," Caleb replied.

"When did you become his mate to defend him like that?" Cornelia asked.

Caleb stared at her weirdly and said, "We must know when we should stop bothering him because his situation is serious now."

Meanwhile, Arya took Arkon and went to the bridge, where she had jumped into the river fifteen years ago. She remembered the exact day.

"Here, I tried to make the worst mistake in my life. It was 10:45 pm on 20 December 2005. I even recognize everything like it happened yesterday. After my father left, I focused on my studies. I studied hard, and I believed what he said before he left. It was not easy to handle everything. My mother was hard dealing with that alone. She suffered alone. She didn't show that. I hated her. First, I thought that she didn't care, but when she died, something in me died with her. Someday in school, it was a normal day, but I felt strange, suffocated; a strange feeling controlled me and prevented me from thinking well. I wondered what the was point of living life alone without anyone, no family, and no purpose, and that feeling led me here to this bridge. I asked myself then, why did God not leave anyone for me? Why God hates me! I called my father and said that if my father would answer my call, then I would consider that a sign from God to save my life. That was my conclusion at that age, and my father's phone was off again, so I decided to punish him in the worst way, and I said, 'I will make you regret it for the rest of your life' and I jumped into the water. And I'm here again, saying goodbye to someone I loved. I came here to know my true feelings toward you. I wanted to make sure that I grew up enough to handle this. Thank you, Arkon, because you have been beside me even for a short time." Arkon hugged her tightly.

On the night of that day, at Nani's booth, she woke up, and she was in a panic. She immediately took her purse and headed to Arya's house. When Arya opened the door for her, Nani was urgent, like something terrible would happen.

"I solved the mystery!" Nani said.

"What?" Arya asked.

"I told you before that I saw you in my dreams." Arya turned inside and ignored her.

"Did you come to talk about that, really! Come, let's go inside and eat something," Arya said.

"You are so annoying. Just listen to me," Nani replied. And she added, "I finally discovered the meaning of the dream."

She told Arya that since she was saying that 'That person' saved her in the dream, she naturally assumed she was talking about Arkon. But that 'but' kept bothering her since she couldn't hear anything after that—until a few minutes ago. She told Arya that what she said was: "That person is the one who saved me. But…the person who saved me will be my death angel." Nani told Arya that it means she's going to die!

Meanwhile, Arkon walked inside the room, and Arya stared at him, terrified.

"What are you talking about?" Arkon asked. Arya remained silent, but Nani told Arya that's not the most shocking part. The twist is that it was not Arkon she was talking about in the dream. "There was an older man…in the dream. You said that he saved you, but then you said that he would be the death…" Then she suddenly stopped in shock when she saw the picture frame in the kitchen. It was the picture of Arya as a child with her father, which Arkon had switched so that it was featured in the frame. She picked up the picture frame and yelled, "This man! Who is this man in the frame? He's the same man that I saw in the dream where you said that he's your death angel…" The doorbell rang and cut the anxiety between them. Arkon went to the iron gate and saw that Van was behind the door. He asked, "Where have you been? I was worried about you."

"I have been busy searching and taking care of some stuff, but I didn't know it would take a lot of time," Van replied.

When they entered inside, the three were staring at each other. Arkon said, "You, Arya's friend, can you leave because I don't have much time with Arya!" Nani was shocked that he just told her to leave her best friend's home, so she took Arya and went out.

"Arya, that means your father wants to kill you!" Nani quaked.

"There is no such thing. It was just a dream!" Arya barked.

"But I saw him clearly. He was your father."

"I know, but that is only in your head; it's not reality. Let's assume that he was really my father. You said earlier that whoever saved me that day in the water was the same who would kill me. How is that possible? He wasn't the person who saved me that day because no one was there. I was alone in the water, and I saved myself," Arya insisted.

"Sorry, I may hurt you by mentioning your father. I'll go now. You better go inside. He looked concerned," Nani quaked. Arya went inside. She went back to the frame, wondering, *Why is this photo in the front!* She looked up as she realized that Arkon had brought the photo in the front.

Up in Arkon's roof room, he sat with Van.

"Did you find what you were looking for?" Arkon asked.

"You can say that, but I didn't find the magical board that can achieve the servant's wish. I found just part of it," Van explained.

"Whatever you have, do it at Caleb's house. Leave. Don't bother me."

"How long do you have here?"

"I have only six days."

"I heard that you went to Meridian and came back. Are you thinking of not going back there? You know that would be the worst thing you do," Van stammered.

"I know that I can't stay here if I decide not to go back," Arkon bawled.

"Okay, I must say goodbye to her," Van stated. They went downstairs, where Arya was changing the photos again, and he saw the picture and clucked his tongue, asking cryptically if the father made the daughter carry his burden.

Van asked Arya gently if she wanted to find him, which upset her. Arkon rushed Van out, then went back to stop Arya from hiding her father's picture. He put it back in the frame, musing that when she said she'd forgotten someone and that she hated them, it meant the opposite, just like everything else she said.

He apologized for not being able to make her wish to see her father come true. He told her to keep trying to find him because even if he was the worst man in the world, she deserved answers. He added that it makes him crazy to think of her still in that darkness after he leaves. She started to cry. She cried because she would come back to be alone again. She used to be busy all the time when Arkon was beside her; he filled her life, and now all that would fade. He approached her and hugged her.

Meanwhile, in Caleb's penthouse, Cornelia was on pins and needles, worried that Arkon would decide not to go back to the realm of Meridian. Caleb assured her that Arkon knows what will happen if he doesn't, certain that he'll leave. Van showed up to report that he didn't find his tablet where he thought it would be but that he knows who took it. Confused, Caleb asked that humans couldn't even see it, but Van countered that some humans could. He asked if he could crash at Caleb's for the night, and both Caleb and Cornelia shouted, "NO!" Then they exchanged awkward glances. Van called Tynar next to ask him to let him into Arya's place. Tynar said that he would be working all night.

In the morning, Arya crept upstairs to find Arkon still sleeping. He surprised her by grabbing her hand and pulling her down next to him. "I was waiting for you to come and wake me up!" He tampered with her hair gently.

"Why?" Arya whispered.

"There is no reason," Arkon stated.

She grinned and stared into his eyes, approached him closely, and said, "I brought you a gift." She got up and walked to the closet, where a neat suit hung.

"I wanted to buy you the best and most expensive gift, but I couldn't find something more expensive than your immortal friend's gifts, so I chose this suit. I hope you will like it. Please wear it on today's date," Arya requested. They spent the day doing simple things like running in the park and playing cutthroat games of rock-paper-scissors. Poor Arkon was terrible at it and suffered countless forehead flicks and wrist smacks from Arya. After they had their lunch,

Arya took him to a historic place full of trees and peaceful sights. And there was a portrait artist. She told Arkon that if he wins a game of rock-paper-scissors against the artist, he will draw their portrait. On the third throw, the artist's wife stepped on her husband's foot and made him lose. Arkon was so amazed that he won.

Something was going on because the wife hustled Arya away, leaving Arkon with the artist. The artist said that his wife and Arkon's bride seemed to have a plan, and Arkon's head whipped around at the word 'bride'.

Arya returned, and when Arkon saw her, he lost every last wit he possessed. She was looking stunning in a wedding dress with a coronet of flowers in her hair, and she approached him then asked if she looked pretty. Speechless, Arkon could only stare at her in wonder. As they sat, Arkon's eyes still locked on Arya. She said that photographs fade. She told Arkon that in this portrait, his face would remain more vivid than in photographs. The artist's wife brought Arya a bouquet of flowers, and Arkon could hardly tear his eyes away from her. He eventually looked up to pose for the portrait, which turned out beautifully.

Meanwhile, Van visited Julian for the first time. He wanted to ask him many questions about the night of the accident nine years ago, when he lost his memory on the same day he met Julian when he first came to the realm of humans.

"I'm sorry because I had to leave you that night, but I was scared, and it was the first time for me in this world," Julian stated.

"No, please don't be sorry; it was an accident, and I totally understand that. Don't think that I'm like the other guards, please. But I'm here because I want to ask you about someone you may know!" Van acknowledged.

"Who?"

"I want to ask you about the identity of the person who saved you that day. I assume that you didn't survive in this world without help. On that day, I lost something magical; it's the tablet of the servant that makes the servant's wish come true, so I went to the accident place. I used my powers to recall that day, and I knew that you were saved by a woman who raised you later. And a man was accompanying her that day," Van explained.

Yes, that's true, but why are you looking for him? Julian wondered.

"It seems that he found that tablet and took it. Did he tell you about his destination or where he went?"

"Actually, yes, he said that he must find someone on that day, but I was tired and confused, so I left with the woman first. Then my mother, the woman who found him, told me that this man was on his way to see his wife's grave, which was near that area. He was coming back after being out of the country for one year, and he got to know about his wife's death recently at the time, and we haven't heard from him since that day. My mother tried to find him, but she couldn't, but I remembered that he wanted to meet someone on that day!"

"Who?" Van asked.

"His daughter," Julian assured.

Van keened and opened his eyes widely and insinuated, "Was his name Olsen?"

"Yes, that's right!" Julian confirmed. Van was in great shock, but he felt that from the beginning. He stood immediately and thanked Julian. Then he vanished and instantly moved to Arya's house.

The three, Arya, Van, and Arkon, stood in Arya's living room.

"On 20 December 2005, where have you been on that date?" Van asked.

"20 December 2005..." She went silent and couldn't answer. Arkon held Van's arm and pulled him upstairs.

"What is this trick? Why did you come back? And why did you ask her about that?" Arkon barked.

"This date was the day of the accident when I lost my powers—"

"And why did you ask her about that? What's her relation to that accident?" Arkon interrupted.

"Her father, Olsen, took my tablet that night!" Van explained.

"What?"

"I was shocked when I knew that too. He's the man who helped Julian. And he also took me to the hospital when I lost my memory that night, and he is Arya's father, which means he's another servant of us; that's why he saw the magical tablet," Van revealed.

Arkon was confused about that coincidence, but he repeated, "Why is that related to Arya?"

Van said that the tablet must have recognized a servant, but Arkon was still confused. Backing up, Van told him that before saving him that night, Arya's father saved Julian and that he'd said he needed to find his daughter, and Arkon remembered that the tablet has the power to grant the servant's most earnest wish. Van continued that the tablet must have taken Arya's father to her.

"That's why I asked Arya about her place that night," Van explained. Arkon hardly received this news. He couldn't think of more than one possibility.

Meanwhile, Arya was holding the picture frame. She was saying, "Come back to see me, and I will forgive you for everything."

He sent Van to see the bridge where Arya had tried to commit suicide.

"This is sorrowful," Van uttered. Then he picked up his phone and called Arkon. "I found him here! As you expected," Van whined.

Arkon put the phone down, and he couldn't know what to do. He went downstairs and saw Arya, who was making a list of things to do with Arkon before he left. She told Arkon brightly that he was right and that she'd keep looking for her father and make him apologize. Arkon couldn't say anything when she said that, so he just said that he had to go out for a bit and that he'd be back soon.

At Julian's office, Julian was thinking about what he learned about Arya's father and how Van asked him not to say anything if he saw Arya. He called Arya and asked her to meet with him.

At the river, Van pointed out to Arkon where Arya's father lay, along with his tablet. He thought that Arya must have survived her fall into the river that night because of her father. Arkon was stricken, remembering how badly Arya wanted to see her father one more time. He said that he's going to get Arya's father out. He dove into the river and tried to get him out.

When Arya arrived at Julian's office, she sat in front of him and asked, "Why did you want to meet me?" Julian told her that this would be his last session and that he was going to tell her the rest of his past. He'd mentioned previously that he followed a light out of the woods the night he came to the human world, which turned out to be a car's headlights. Cowering on the road, Julian had been terrified. Arya's father had covered him with his jacket and hugged him, saying that it would be okay. Julian told Arya that it was the first time he'd felt the warmth of a human body and learned the power of someone saying, "It's okay."

He said that if that man hadn't been the first person he'd met that night— someone who told him it was okay and hugged him—he wouldn't know what he would have become. He told Arya that he'd met three gods in his life—that man, his stepmother, and Arya herself. He asked to thank her with a handshake, and she readily held out her hand with a smile. She didn't realize that he was talking about her father.

When she came back to her home, she saw Arkon standing in front of their portrait. She approached him and saw that his shirt was wet. She asked, "What's wrong?" She approached him closely and repeated, "What's happened with you? You look sad."

He remained silent for several moments, then spoke, "Your father…I found him!"

"Where? Where is he now?" Arya stammered.

"In the river bottom where you jumped into years ago!"

"What? What are you saying?"

"On that day, he came back when he knew that your mother had died; he was on his way to her grave, but he met Van on the way to the accident, and he saw the magical tablet that makes the servant's wish come true, and his wish on that day was to see you, so the tablet transferred him to the bridge, and he saw you jumping off the bridge, so he jumped after you, which means he saved you, and you didn't realize that."

Arkon took Arya to the river's edge, where she collapsed, crying. She started to scream, "Dad! Dad! Come out, please…" Arya clutched at Arkon, begging him to save her father, wailing that he couldn't die like this. He hugged her tightly.

"Arkon, please save him; you are immortal, and you have magical powers. Please do something," Arya begged.

Arkon felt something; a voice inside his ears whispered, "Meridian…the Jewel of Meridian." Arkon turned left and right, but he saw nothing, while Arya was still requesting, "Save my dad; bring him back to life!"

"I can't. No one can bring people back from death."

"I was a fool. I didn't know. I thought I got out alone from the water. I killed him. He died because of me," Arya sobbed.

She blamed herself for spending so many years hating him. Arkon held her, repeating that it was not her fault. She tried to follow her father into the water, convinced that he was there waiting for her to save him. Arkon held her back, begging her not to do this as she fought and screamed.

Meanwhile, Van was in Caleb's penthouse, explaining to Caleb and Cornelia that Arkon tried to retrieve Arya's father's body, but it wouldn't move from its resting place at the bottom of the river. He told them that his body was perfectly preserved because of the tablet, so Arkon left the tablet there.

"Why is his body stuck there?" Cornelia asked.

"I don't know why. It's somehow magical, but it's beyond our powers," Van replied.

Arkon stayed up all night, keeping vigil as Arya slept. He thought about Arya when she said that a king is a being that grants a human being's deepest wishes, feeling helpless to do anything for her now. He never took his eyes off her until Tynar found him the next morning and called him up to the roof.

Caleb and Cornelia were there, as was Van. Caleb told Arkon that he and Cornelia also tried to retrieve Arya's father's body, but it wouldn't move for them either. Arkon told them that Arya wanted to go after him herself, but Cornelia asked why they couldn't just leave him there. She grew angry, reminding Arkon that she's known him for millennia and that she knows what he's thinking. She said that Arkon is planning to use his one burst of power to help Arya instead of using it to open the magical gate to get himself home.

Arkon's silence was all the confirmation they needed, and everyone objected. They reminded Arkon that he'd die if he didn't go back to the world of Meridian. They all refused to allow it, but Arkon told them that Arya believes it's a king's duty to protect humans.

"First, you wasted your time with this human girl, and you lost the last chance to find the jewel, and now you are trying to lose your life for her sake. What's wrong with you?" Cornelia barked.

He asked them, "How can I call myself a prince if I can't save one woman?" Cornelia countered that Arya wouldn't want this, and she added that if Arkon dies, he'll disappear from the memories of humans, including Arya. Before he could respond, they all turned at a noise. It was Arya, who ignored them to stare incredulously at Arkon. She asked him what that meant, but he couldn't look her in the eye. He followed her inside, where she cried again.

She sobbed, "How can you think of doing such a cruel thing to me? Are you going to die? Will you disappear from my memory? I'll forget about you for the rest of my life?"

Arkon pleaded with her to understand that it's because he's been unable to do anything for her. He begged her to give him a chance to grant her a wish as a king and to let him keep his promise to protect her. Arya sobbed, saying that she never asked him to sacrifice his life for her.

Frantic, Cornelia desperately searched for a way to make Arkon go back to the realm of Meridian, but Caleb said they can't force a king to do anything. Cornelia ordered him to use his own powers to help Arya, but he reminded her that none of them have enough power to do that. So Caleb talked to Arya, telling her what would happen if Arkon didn't go back to Meridian. He explained that

Arkon exists for one purpose—to be king—so if he doesn't become king and stay here, there's no reason for him to exist. And he would fade. Caleb asked Arya to tell Arkon that she's willing to leave her father where he is. To make Arkon go back to Meridian.

She agreed, and Arkon told her that he'd been selfish by asking her to live with her memories of him. He made her promise that she'd cherish her life after he left, and he said that her father would be at peace where he was. Arkon swore that, as the prince of Meridian, he'd look after her forever, even if he was not with her. He asked Arya to go with him to see her father, and he took her back to the river's edge. She apologized to her father over and over, so Arkon told her not to worry. She answered that they were just following their original plan and asked where they should go now.

Arkon just held her hand and looked at her sadly. He whispered, "I love you," and kissed her. But his kiss was desperate, and Arya sensed something was wrong, and she tried to push him away. When Arkon finally broke the kiss, he told her that the kiss was a graceful kiss, bidding her to live a happy and full life. Arya started to panic, realizing that he had just given her his power, understanding dawning that it was too late to reverse it.

Arkon calmly told Arya to find someone to love and live her life in happiness. A tear slid down his cheek as he said that happiness is what she's always wanted the most, but Arya refused to listen, accusing him of planning this all along. He hugged her fiercely and said that he couldn't leave without doing anything for her because he knew she'd go to her father and die after he left. Arya fought with him, calling him foolish, and asked what she was supposed to do now. Arkon told her to go to her father now. He requested one last time.

"Let me do something for you while I'm still here."

Caleb, Cornelia, and Van materialized nearby, and they instantly sensed that they were too late to stop Arkon. Cornelia buried her head into Caleb's shoulder as Arkon told Arya to go. Finally, she accepted his decision. Arya dove into the water, with Arkon following right behind. With Arkon's power, Arya didn't need to breathe as she swam deep to the bottom of the river, where her father's body lay. He almost looked alive, protected by a magical veil of power created by the tablet, and it was still in his pocket. When Arkon used the only remaining power to help Arya, he lost the chance to go back to Meridian because this power was only to open the magical gate.

Arya looked at her father, asking why he was here all alone and why he didn't call her sooner. She took his hand. His body raised easily at her touch. Arya pulled him to the surface, saved by his daughter, as he once had saved her.

Chapter Eleven
Throne but Love

Arya had her father's body laid to rest under a tree, and she promised to bring her mother here too, in time. Arkon was still with her, his time in the human world not yet up, and as he hugged Arya, she said sweetly that she was never going to forgive him. She promised to hate and resent him and to regret meeting him because he sacrificed his chance to go back to Meridian and even his last chance to live, and he agreed to it all.

"Do you think that I will let you die?" Arya said.

"What do you mean?" Arkon asked.

Then, Cornelia, Caleb, Van, and Tynar showed up behind them, and Van was holding the magical tablet that was with her father.

Then Arya told Arkon that she was going to put everything back to normal before any of that happened! Arkon repeated, "What do you mean?"

But it was Cornelia who spoke up. "I thought she was stupid, but I guess she was smart enough to think of this."

They turned to see all of their friends there, and Tynar giggled that Arya had come up with a solution to their problem, and Arya told Arkon that she was going to use her wish to help him return to the realm of Meridian. Cornelia urged them to hurry before she gave in to her desire to kill them both.

Van gave her the magical tablet, and a luminous ray filled the place with Arya's wish. Arkon tried to open a gate and waved with his hands, and the gate opened. Cornelia smiled, and Arya was about to cry because the time had come to leave her love, but Arkon turned to her and everybody and said, "I'm not going anywhere! I was ready to die here beside the woman I love. I don't want to go back. My place is here beside you, even if I die."

He approached Arya and kissed her. Cornelia yelled at him, "What are you doing? This is the last chance for you!"

Suddenly, a tremendous and gleaming light came out of Arya's chest. Arya's necklace flew into the air, and everyone watched in shock. The necklace transformed in the air into another shape, a great green jewel with massive amount of light waves scattered around. And Tynar shouted, "Everyone bow now. It's the Great Jewel of Meridian!"

Everyone bowed in front of the jewel, and Arya was speechless, and Arkon was staring in amazement. Van uttered, "Halinor was right. The prophecy is real!"

"What prophecy?" Cornelia asked.

FLASHBACK – VAN'S TRIP

On Van's trip to search for the tablet, he came back to the accident's place in the woods. He was searching for the tablet when a voice spoke from behind.

"You should not search here!"

"Who is that? Show yourself," Van stated.

Halinor came out, and when Van first saw her, he bowed his head and said, "Lady Halinor, it is a great honor to see you."

"Good to see you too, Van. I came here to tell you something. There was an ancient prophecy about an immortal prince who fell in love with a human girl, and this girl would be different from the other humans because this human girl would have the trust of the heart of the universe. I mean the Great Jewel of Meridian, and she will be the end of the world's suffering. Do you know what I mean?"

"Yes, I realized that girl was different, but I couldn't know why until this moment. What do you need me to do?" Van asked.

"You should go and search for the man who saved you!" Halinor replied.

"How? And why?" Van asked. But Halinor was gone.

END FLASHBACK

Everyone was shocked when and why the jewel was with Arya. In the meantime, the jewel finally settled in the hand of the heir. He did not fully understand what happened, but he remembered Queen Wera's words: Do what your heart tells you to do. Meanwhile, a magical gate opened in front of them, and Queen Wera with Halinor came out of it. Everyone bowed to the queen. She approached them and said, "You took a lot of time to realize the truth. The jewel shows itself only when you are your true self, Your Majesty. This girl is unique. When the jewel was sent to earth, it chose Arya as the safest place on earth because of her heart. This girl has the purest heart in this world. That's why it chose her, and you were blind, but finally, you realized what you really want."

She hugged him and said, "The new king of the great world, I'm really proud to be your mother."

Then Halinor approached Arya and caught her hand. Arya uttered, "You! You are the woman who gave me the stone!"

Arkon was surprised and wondered, *What? Halinor!*

"Yes, that's true. I hope I was a good driver for you! And a good librarian!" Halinor revealed.

"What? Oh my God. You were all those people who helped me. And you are wearing the same ring. I can't believe that."

Queen Wera looked at Arkon and said, "You are free now to do whatever you want to do."

Arkon flew into the air. He was missing his powers quite much and stated, "I'm the heir of Meridian and the king of the Great World. I call all the veil guards wherever they are. Come now and be in my presence."

The three, Cornelia, Caleb, and Van, were already there, and another two came immediately with the instant transmission. The five guards of the veil were there. So Arkon declared, "I give the guards their freedom to be back to their normal lives, and there are no veil guards anymore. I will stay in this world, and I will protect the veil on my own, and I will save this world from its misery with the great powers of mine, and you are free to choose your place to stay."

He landed on the ground and ordered, "I order all the gates everywhere to close themselves, and the gates will open only by the chosen people."

Cornelia was delighted that she would finally be free with Caleb to do whatever they wanted to do, and they thanked their king.

Three months later, on Adalar Island, King Arkon and his wife Arya sat in a hot water lake on a high hill in their palace. They were pondering the stars at night. Arya said, "I understand now why you loved the hot water lakes. I love you, my king."

"I love you, my queen." He kissed her.

Then Arya said, "I wonder how our kids will be. And what will their journey look like? I want to write them a book. I want to tell them the great story of an immortal king who came from a very faraway world, loved a human girl, and chose to live with her in her world."

People can survive anything with the strength they have. But if that strength were love, it would be even better.